The Song of the Froom

By Stella Wulf

www.stellawulf.com

Copyright © Stella Wulf 2011

Cover & illustrations copyright © Claire Jefferson 2011

Published by Stella Wulf

For those who keep the magic alive;
Abigail, Tabitha, Jessica, Jack & Adam.

Map of the Wide River Valley

One

The Arrival of Spring

Spring is here
Spring is cheer
Twister your whiskers
Untangle your hair
Frisker your tails and twingle your toes
Come out and sniff the new blown rose
Wake up, get up for Spring has sprung
Trimble your trotters, come join the song
Patter your paws, come sing along
For Spring is now and Spring is cheer
Spring is heeeeeeeeeeeeeeeeeerreeee!!!

Piper Froom opened his eyes, poked his long velvet snout from his cozy bed of leaves and sniffed the air. Something was terribly wrong. That last high note of Pa's that had always soared so beautifully and unswervingly, had faltered, stumbled and finally screeched to a juddering halt.

Piper lay staring at the roof of his burrow as the horrible realization made his heart race and his stomach lurch. Pa's discordant note had filled him with a feeling of dread and for the first time in his life he was in no hurry to leave his bed.

Oh I wish I could just go back to sleep and never wake up, he thought desperately. He'd hoped that his father would feel better after his Long Winter Sleep but that final, screeching note had said it all. Pa had given his last performance.

The role of 'Eminent Singer' had passed down through the Froom family for generations and the Spring Wake-up Song was the most important of their repertoire. It roused the creatures of the Wide River Valley, gently and serenely from their Long Winter Sleep. Without the song of the Froom to wake them they might have slept through to Midsummers eve!

Piper buried himself deeper into his bed and tried to block out the fearful thoughts that threatened to overwhelm him. *If only I were braver*, he thought wistfully. Ma always said he wouldn't say boo to a weevil. Now the role of 'Eminent Singer' had passed to him! He would be a laughingstock!

A hot flush of shame suddenly engulfed him as his mind went back to that awful day when his guilty secret had been discovered.

It was the eve of the Long Winter Sleep and he'd gone to collect nuts for the autumn feast. Piper always tried out his voice when he was alone, (he was far too shy ever to try to sing in company). As usual he'd attempted a few hesitant and quavering notes in the hope that a miracle might have happened. The strangled squeak that escaped from his mouth had surprised even him. He'd cleared his throat and tried again, this time with even more alarming results. That's when Snorky Trotter and his swinish gang had burst from the bushes laughing and jeering. 'Hah, hah, hah! The Froom can't sing! What a loser! Piper's a loser,

Piper's a loser,' they'd taunted. Then they'd shoved him in the bushes and run off squealing and snorting with delight at the revelation. Piper's secret was out.

It didn't matter that none of the other creatures of the Lumbery Wood could sing. Indeed, Snorky Trotter had a voice like the scraping of claws on dry slate but nobody cared about that. It is the Froom who is graced with the most beautiful voice of any living creature and his song spreads joy and hope throughout the land. Piper was a Froom. He was born to sing. It wasn't surprising then, that when he'd tried to tell his father he couldn't sing Pa had dismissed the idea as idiotic. 'What nonsense Piper, of course you can sing! All Frooms can sing! It's what we do! Your Grandpa could shatter conkers with his voice. His famous high note once burst the eardrums of a Vishis Fween! It's a great honour to sing the Wake-up Song Piper and you are the next in line. You'll just have to find your voice so let's hear no more about this foolishness.' Piper had gone to sleep with those words ringing in his ears.

A rush of panic suddenly overtook him and he threw aside his leafy cover and came spluttering up for air. The news will be all over the Lumbery Wood by now, Snorky Trotter will have seen to that! 'Piper Froom can't sing! Whoever heard of a Froom that can't sing?' they'll all be saying. *I can't face them! I'll have to run away!* he thought frantically. The idea came to him with a stab of pain and relief. *Yes, that's it! I'll run away and I won't come back until I've found my voice!*

Outside the Froom burrow the tall trees unfolded their delicate buds and basked in the warmth of the shy young sun. Spring began to hum with expectation and excitement as the inhabitants of the Lumbery Wood began a yawning and a stretching, a scratching of ears and a rubbing of noses, a twiskering of whiskers and a friskering of tails. Piper crawled from his burrow, hardly daring to acknowledge the terrifying thought that had just occurred to him.

As he poked his nose outside and sniffed the warm spring air which usually filled him with joy and excitement, all he could think was, *why me? Why do I have to be the only Froom on earth who can't sing?*

Ma had been humming softly to herself as she tidied away the winter bedding. As Piper emerged from the burrow she smiled anxiously at him. 'Did you sleep well?' she asked gently. Until now Piper's inability to sing had been their unspoken secret.

'You'd better shake a leg,' she said, quickly changing the subject. 'Pa will be wondering where you've got to.' Piper sighed and plodded off to meet his father who was on his way back from Noggin Hill. As Pa approached, Piper could see that he was visibly shaken by his near failure that morning but he was trying hard not to show it.

'Phew,' puffed Pa, 'I feel quite exhausted.' They trotted along in awkward silence before Pa caught his breath and uttered the words that Piper dreaded to hear. 'How about it Piper, do you remember what we talked about before the Long Winter Sleep?' Piper had thought about nothing else but Pa's trembling paws and the frightened look in his eyes made him panic.

'Don't worry Pa, I'll do my best to find my voice,' he blurted out. Then he added, with as much conviction as he could, 'I won't let you down.'

'That's my boy,' said Pa with undisguised relief. 'Now, lets have breakfast. I'm famished!'

Oh my trimbly trotters, thought Piper, dismayed at his rash words. *How on earth am I going to find my voice and where am I going to start looking? And if I do find it will I ever have the courage to stand on Noggin Hill and sing the Spring Wake-up Song?*

Two

Piper's Quest

Piper knew how much Ma loved that first delicious day of spring that held so much promise. She always said that waking to Pa's melodious notes filled her with love and wellbeing. All through breakfast she'd kept up her usual cheerful appearance, pretending that nothing out of the ordinary had happened, but she'd sighed wistfully with every glance at Piper. The burden of responsibility was beginning to weigh heavily on him but the idea of running away terrified him. He wasn't sure if he was more afraid to go or more afraid to stay.

As he struggled with his mixed emotions, there came a dreadful commotion from the treetops. The slender boughs began a swaying and a cracking as a large yellow bird crashed its way through the branches and came flapping and cursing into their midst.

'Vladivostokkkkkkkk!' it squawked.

'That'll be Pierre right on time,' said Ma nervously as the old Chisel-beaked Stonepecker crash landed on the ground in front of them, scattering the remains of their breakfast in every direction.

'Happy Spring Babushkas,' he screeched as he picked himself up and shook out his ruffled feathers. (He liked to pepper his conversation with foreign words even though he didn't always know what they meant. He thought it made him appear very clever and important).

Pierre had spent many years in foreign parts chiseling, hollowing, pecking and hammering and it had fuddled his brain and disrupted his flying. He was well travelled and knew the Wide River Valley like the back of his wing. Nowadays, he made a career out of being a busybody and telling tall stories and he considered it his professional obligation to be up to date with all the latest gossip.

Pa was squirming with embarrassment and Ma was fidgeting nervously knowing that the sole topic of conversation that morning would be the discordance of the Spring Wake-up Song.

I'll have to distract him before he upsets Pa, thought Piper in a panic. 'What's the news Pierre? Have we missed anything while we've been sleeping?' he said before Pierre could open his beak.

'The news is . . . while you've been sleeping? Oh, well now darlings, let me see; while you've been asleep? . . . Oh yes! The Flox's have renovated their den and added two more bedrooms . . . and the Spoonbills have just got back from their winter holiday in South Island and have started building their nests; and the Magpies have squabbled all winter - nothing new there! . . . Umm . . . what else? Oh yes, the Beavers have moved back into The Old Lodge and . . . ' As Pierre chattered on, giving the low-down on the doings of the entire Wide River Valley, Piper was frantically searching his mind for a solution.

Oh, what am I going to do? Pa's going to find out sooner or later that I REALLY can't sing! I can't let him down. He stared miserably at his parents.

Pa was still twitching with anxiety but Piper could see that Ma's attention had wandered. He knew that she wasn't interested in anything outside the safe, comfortable world of the Lumbery Wood. Whenever Grandpa tried to talk of his adventures Ma would give him a look hard enough to crack a hazelnut! Poor Grandpa would sigh resignedly and plod off back to his own burrow.

'And Grunter Bog-hog snored so loudly that his roof caved in!' exclaimed the old Stonepecker, chortling with delight.

Maybe Pierre could help me, thought Piper, his heart suddenly leaping with hope. *After all, he's been everywhere and done everything. He's sure to know something!*

'Yes, yes, it's all been happening while you've been asleep. Now then, what was it I was going to tell you?' he said, stroking his beak thoughtfully.

'I'm sure Mrs Peeble is dying to hear what the Flox's have been up to,' said Piper hurriedly.

'Quite right darlings, I can't stand here chatting all day, the Peebles will be waiting.' As Pierre prepared to leave Ma suddenly remembered something.

'Is there any news of the Soozles?' she asked.

'Ah, the poor Soozles; quite slipped my mind but I'm afraid not,' replied Pierre, shaking his head. 'Nobody's seen hide nor hair of them.' Piper suddenly felt ashamed. *Oh no! I've been so busy worrying about my own problems, I'd quite forgotten that Snoot's parents are missing. He'll be wondering where I am*, he thought guiltily.

'Wait for me Pierre, I'll walk with you,' Piper said to the old Stonepecker who was straightening his feathers in readiness for his visit to the Peebles. 'Is it all right Ma? I want to check on Snoot.'

'Of course dear,' said Ma. 'I'm sure poor Snoot will be eager to see you.'

Snoot Soozle was Piper's best friend. His parents Cracker and Stasha, had disappeared on the night of the Great Storm when they'd gone out foraging for snails and they hadn't been seen since. Piper was eager to see his friend but this was also his chance to speak to Pierre alone.

As soon as they were out of sight of the Froom burrow and before the old bird could start chatting again, Piper seized his opportunity.

'Ummm . . . Pierre? I was wondering if you knew anything about . . . voices?' he asked shyly.

'Voices dearie? What kind of voices?' asked Pierre, surprised at the question.

'Singing voices! Lost voices!' Piper exclaimed. It had come to him in a flash that if a voice could be found then it must first be lost. 'I was just wondering, that's all,' he added casually so as not to arouse Pierre's suspicions.

Pierre threw back his head, squinted at the sky and stroked his beak thoughtfully before replying. He loved to tell stories and this was a golden opportunity.

'Well Bambino,' he whispered secretively. 'It just so happens that there *are* lost Voices out there. Angelic singing Voices! Enchanting, spellbinding Voices that wander the land in search of a worthy host. Legend has it that they're hunted down by the evil Fweens and imprisoned on Mount Florn. The Vishis Fween is obsessed with the rapturous Voices and guards them day and night.' Pierre was warming nicely to his story and beginning to get into his stride. 'It is said that on the night of the full moon, the Voices sing so entrancingly and so mesmerizingly that the Vishis Fween and his tribe are forced to leave the Mountain for fear of losing their minds.'

'But why are they in fear of losing their minds?' interrupted Piper who'd been listening agog.

'Because . . . because . . . well because they know they're not worthy! Such loathsome beasts would become completely unhinged by the beauty and purity of those Voices! Now where was I? Oh yes . . .' he went on mysteriously. 'It is only on the night of the full moon when they are left unguarded that the Voices can be set free by anyone worthy (or brave) enough to claim them.'

Just then Freda Peeble appeared on the path up ahead and Pierre suddenly lost interest in the tale.

'Hi there, Freda!' he called out to her. 'Got to go dear,' he said hurriedly to Piper. 'Places to go, Peebles to see,' and he scurried off to catch up on the latest gossip, chuckling with glee at his little joke.

So that's it! thought Piper who'd been enthralled by Pierre's story. *That must be Grandpa's secret. He's always trying to tell me things and he did have the most beautiful and enchanting voice of any living Froom. All I have to do is go to Mount Florn on the night of the full moon and rescue a Voice; my Voice!* Piper was excited and dismayed, all at the same time. His thoughts in a turmoil, he finally arrived at Snoot's burrow where his friend was waiting for him.

'There you are,' said Snoot, 'I wondered where you'd got to. I was worried about you, what with your Pa's wobbly note and everything.'

Piper and Snoot were as different as acorns and apples. Snoot was outgoing and confident and if he'd been a Froom he'd have had no trouble in standing on Noggin

Hill and singing the Spring Wake-up Song. Until the Snorky Trotter episode apart from Ma, Snoot had been the only other creature that knew of Piper's secret. He was aware of his friend's shyness but like Ma, he thought Piper had plenty of time to overcome his difficulties. 'Stop worrying about it Piper! You'll grow out of your shyness and your un-Froomish voice will become Froomish in the fullness of time, you'll see,' Snoot had reassured him. No one had expected that Pa's voice would give out so early on in his term, after all Grandpa had carried on singing until well into his hoary years. It seemed to Piper that time had already reached its fullness and he still didn't have a voice, Froomish or otherwise.

'Oh I'm all right, really Snoot don't worry about me,' bluffed Piper, mindful that his friend had just spent his first winter alone. 'How about you?'

'Oh, you know; so, so,' Snoot replied bravely. 'It's not the first time my parents have gone missing. But are you really all right Piper? I've never seen you this agitated before.'

'I'm running away Snoot! After-this-morning's-performance-it's-obvious-that-Pa-can't-carry-on-and-I-have-to-take-over-the-Spring-Wake-up-Song-and-now-everyone-knows-I-can't-sing-so-I'm-going-to-Mount-Florn-to-find-my-Voice-which-is-being-held-prisoner-by-the-Fweens,' Piper blurted out.

'Whoa, whoa! What are you talking about? You can't run away! And what's all this nonsense about voices and Mount Florn and Fweens?' demanded Snoot incredulously. Piper sighed and flopped heavily onto the ground outside Snoot's burrow. Snoot threw himself down alongside his friend as Piper recounted Pierre's story.

'So you see, if I am to take over the Spring Wake-up Song I have to go to Mount Florn and rescue my Voice,' he said finally.

'Wow!' said Snoot, his eyes shining with excitement. 'That's quite a story.'

'So what do you think then?' asked Piper tentatively.

'Why are we still here?' cried Snoot enthusiastically. 'The moon is already waxing. It can't be long now until it reaches its zenith. We'd better get a move on, it's a long way to Mount Florn!'

'Do you really mean it Snoot? You'll run away with me?'

'I prefer to think of it as . . . A QUEST!' Snoot said decidedly. 'You'll be needing my navigating skills if we're heading off into the unknown.'

Piper grinned with relief that his friend was going with him on 'the quest' but his expression didn't reflect what he was feeling inside. He didn't have an adventurous spirit. He loved his home in the Lumbery Wood and he wasn't ready to leave Ma and Pa just yet, but what choice did he have? He had to find his Voice, there was too much at stake. As for Snoot, as far as Piper was aware (and he'd known him all his life), apart from the odd foray with his parents he'd hardly set foot outside his own burrow. How on earth was he going to navigate a course all the way to Mount Florn?

'There's no time to lose,' said Snoot, impatient to get started now that they had a quest. 'If we leave now we could reach the Wide River before nightfall.'

'What, right now? This minute?' gasped Piper in horror. The terrifying thought of running away (or as Snoot put it, going on a quest) had only occurred to him that morning. He wasn't expecting to take off just like that, with no preparation!

'There's no time like the present,' said Snoot. Piper knew that Snoot was right. If he didn't act now he would lose his nerve completely. He had no idea how far it was to Mount Florn or how they were going to get there but Snoot was fired up and ready to go.

'But . . . but . . . what about Ma and Pa? I can't just go! Can I?'

'Well, you can't tell them what you're planning to do that's for sure! You know what your Ma thinks about adventuring Frooms. *It's not natural! Frooms are made for singing, not adventuring,*' Snoot mimicked in his best Ma Froom voice. 'She won't even let Grandpa tell you his stories!'

'It's true that she's always been disapproving of Grandpa but I never really knew why,' said Piper thoughtfully. 'He must have had adventures because Pa told me he'd once burst the eardrums of a Vishis Fween.' Piper sighed. 'Perhaps you're right. There's nothing to be gained by putting it off.'

'It's now or never Piper,' said Snoot enthusiastically.

'Onwards and upwards then,' said Piper unconvincingly. Snoot didn't need any more encouragement and he set off at a rare old pace, whistling happily to himself. *Whatever have I got myself into?* Piper thought as he scuttled along behind. *I've barely had time to think about it and my journey . . . my quest . . . has already begun!*

'Mount Florn lies due south of the Lumbery Wood,' Snoot announced between whistles. 'If we can cross the

Wide River before nightfall, we'll be well and truly on our way.'

'I'm already further from home than I've ever been,' Piper squeaked.

'It's an adventure Piper!' Snoot said chirpily. 'Besides, I can't sit and wait any longer for my parents to come home. I need to do something.'

After a while Snoot ceased his whistling and settled into an easier pace. They walked in silence, each lost in his own thoughts. *I wish I were like Snoot,* Piper thought longingly. *He's so brave and undaunted. But I've taken the first step,* he reassured himself. *I'm on my way to finding my Voice!* Piper felt his determination beginning to grow. Grandpa always said that Piper's determination was his greatest strength. 'You're just like your Grandpa,' his mother would say when he'd made up his mind to do something. But somehow the way she said it always made him feel it was a bad thing. Despite his determination Piper was on unfamiliar territory and it made him anxious.

'A hazelnut for your thoughts,' said Snoot finally breaking the silence.

'I was just thinking that I've never been outside the Lumbery Wood and I don't mind telling you Snoot, that the thought of it terrifies me.'

'I have to admit that the thought quite excites me,' Snoot replied.

'It must be in your blood, your parents being nomads and everything,' said Piper.

'I guess so, but I don't think they'd approve of me going off adventuring. They spent their whole lives moving from one place to another and when I was born, they wanted to give me a better life, that's why they settled here in the Lumbery wood. They never could resist going off on expeditions though,' he added sadly.

'They've always come back sooner or later,' said Piper.

'But they've never stayed away this long before Piper. I'm afraid this time, something terrible might have happened to them.'

'We'll find them Snoot, don't you worry!' said Piper reassuringly.

'We'll find them both,' said Snoot rallying. Your Voice and my parents! Look Piper, there's the river.'

Ahead of them lay the reedy banks of the Wide River. 'Oh my frisky whiskers!' Piper exclaimed. 'I didn't expect it to be so . . . WIDE.' He gazed in awe at the vast expanse of water then looked back longingly at the Lumbery Wood. He breathed in the earthy scent and basked in the comforting familiarity.

'What a sight!' cried Snoot excitedly.

The tall trees stopped at the water's edge and dipped their sinewy toes into the rushing water. The swirling current lapped and licked at the dangling limbs before rushing off on its way through the Gorge of Gulch, past the Tangly Wood to the sea and the white, chalk cliffs. The Wide River had begun its journey far away on Mount Florn where its waters poured from the Thundering Falls in a foamy cascade and tumbled down the mountainside. At the foot of Mount Florn it pulled itself together after its heady, breathless descent and began an idle meander across the Flornean Plain to the Hills of Drumlin. Here it regained its force and rushed its way back to the sinewy toes of the tall trees where the two friends intended to cross its waters. Swelled by the spring rain the swirling current seethed within the confines of its distant banks.

The two small figures stood transfixed in wonder, silhouetted in the pearly glow of the sun as it began its lazy descent to the West.

'What a sight indeed,' Piper exclaimed, but how are we going to get across?'

Snoot looked around in surprise. He scanned the river bank with his sharp, bright eyes then shook his head, perplexed.

'But there should be a bridge, just about here where we're standing. I've been here with my parents Piper and there was definitely a bridge right here,' he insisted.

'What are we going to do now?' said Piper. The friends stared in dismay at the distant bank. It would soon be dark and if they didn't find a way across before nightfall they might as well give up and go home. Snoot would be no closer to finding his parents and as for Piper? He knew there was no turning back. His Voice was waiting for him on Mount Florn. Somehow or other they had to find a way.

Three

Betula and the Beavers

Despite his valiant intentions and determination, Piper felt a little twinge of relief somewhere deep inside himself. Something that said to him, *well never mind, you did your best. Now let's forget all this nonsense and go home.* Then he thought of Ma and Pa and Snorky Trotter and he knew he couldn't go back.

The far bank of the Wide River and the path that would lead their journey onwards, might as well have been on the other side of the world. 'Oh I wish I'd learned to swim,' said Piper in exasperation.

'Me too,' agreed Snoot, 'but I don't think that would help us much. The current's far too strong, we'd be swept away.'

Not knowing what to do next, the two of them stood gazing intently at the river as if hoping to find an answer in the churning swell. 'Maybe we could build a new bridge,' ventured Snoot, 'or a boat,' he said, casting around for inspiration.

'Or maybe we could grow wings and fly across!' retorted Piper. 'Let's face it Snoot, it's hopeless!' he said defeatedly as he threw himself down on the riverbank. Snoot continued to pace up and down in search of a solution. *I don't know what he thinks he's going to find,* thought Piper as he sat watching. Then Snoot stopped abruptly and turned over a large rock that had been thrown up by the turbulent current. Piper had seen him do this many times when he was foraging for snails and he knew it was an instinctive act, *but still,* he thought to himself, *how can he think about food at a time like this?* Suddenly, Snoot let out a cry.

'What's wrong Snoot?' cried Piper rushing to his friend's side.

'My Parents! What if they came here on the night of the Great Storm? The Wide River's the best place to find snails. What if the bridge was washed away with them on it?'

'Your parents are experienced travellers Snoot, they could have gone anywhere,' said Piper reassuringly. 'Besides, why would they come here on a stormy night?'

'You're right Piper. What am I thinking? There are plenty of other good foraging grounds around the Lumbery Wood.' Heartened by this thought, Snoot cracked open a large snail and began to munch distractedly while Piper resumed his contemplation of the watery obstacle. *This is hopeless,* he thought dejectedly. *There's no bridge and neither of us can swim. Unless a miracle happens, it looks like this is the end of my quest and I'll never find my Voice.* Tears of frustration and disappointment began to well up in Piper's eyes. Despite his early reluctance for the quest he found he now wanted it more than ever.

As he brooded over his misfortune a brown, whiskery head suddenly broke the surface of the water and bobbed up and down in front of him. Piper leaped backwards, squealing in surprise and sent Snoot sprawling to the ground.

'What ho,' said the whiskery head, 'I thought I heard voices. Sorry if I startled you! Well, bless me, I haven't seen a Froom around these parts in many a moon. What brings you youngsters to this neck of the woods?'

'We're trying to get across the river,' said Snoot, disentangling himself from his friend.

'Yes,' said Piper loudly, brushing away his tears and trying to hide his embarrassment. 'We're on our way to Mount Florn to rescue my Voice.' The eyes in the head opened wide with horror.

'Oh I wouldn't go there if I were you! Bless my soul, no! I wouldn't even venture to cross this river! No, no, no, I'd go straight back home. Yes, that's what I'd do, straight back home! There are weasels out there and ferrets don't you know! Sneaky little blighters they are. Believe you me, you wouldn't want to find yourselves in a ferret camp!'

With that parting shot the head disappeared abruptly under the water. Moments later the creature to which the whiskery head belonged, pulled its sturdy brown body and long, flat tail, up onto the river bank and plopped down alongside the friends.

'Gnawberry Beaver, how-do-you-do,' he said grinning widely, exposing his long, chisel like teeth. Neither Piper nor Snoot had ever seen a beaver before as the Lodge had not been inhabited since before they were born.

'Piper Froom and Snoot Soozle, very pleased to meet you,' said Piper who had by this time regained his composure. 'Haven't you just moved into the Old Lodge?'

'Goodness me, how did you know that?' asked Gnawberry.

'Pierre!' chimed Piper and Snoot in unison.

'Aah, the old Stonepecker yes, likes to chat! The Lodge, goodness me yes; well me and my good lady wife,

Gnawra are fixing it up. The water rats left the place in a terrible mess; riddled with holes it is. We're busy, busy, busy trying to get the place ship shape.' He leaned in closer and whispered confidentially; 'we might soon be hearing the splashing of tiny paws! But enough about me. What's all this about rescuing a voice? It seems to me that you already have one,' he said, turning to Piper.

'Well . . . you see, next year it's my turn to sing the Spring Wake-up Song. The problem is that I can't sing so I'm going to Mount Florn to rescue my Voice. Pierre told me all about the Voices imprisoned in the cave of the Vishis Fween and I have to get there on the night of the full moon when they'll be left unguarded. It's my quest,' explained Piper. Gnawberry listened thoughtfully.

'Well, Pierre must know what he's talking about, a well travelled old bird like him! But Mount Florn! A dangerous place by all accounts with those evil Fweens everywhere! One snap of those fearsome jaws! Ughhh!' Gnawberry Beaver shuddered with horror. 'Hmm . . . the Spring Wake-up Song, well now! That's an important job,' he reflected. 'A very important job indeed! If there's no Spring Wake-up Song . . . I dread to think what might happen. Yes, yes, I quite see that you're right. You really must find your Voice!'

'But we have to get across the river before nightfall,' said Piper suddenly aware that the afternoon light was fading to a rosy pink. 'Snoot thinks there used to be a bridge here.'

'And so there was,' Gnawberry replied. 'Your friend is quite correct, but it was swept away in the Great Storm.'

Snoot looked at Piper as if to say I told you so. 'Was anybody hurt? Did you see it happen?' he asked, trying to conceal his anxiety.

'Afraid not. It happened before we arrived,' said Gnawberry. The river burst its banks just about here where we are sitting. The place was a disaster area! Debris strewn all over. But wait a minute! That gives me an idea! I think I might just be able to help you.'

He let out a long, shrill whistle and a moment later another brown, whiskery head popped to the surface. 'Meet my wife, Gnawra,' he said. 'Come on old girl, no time to lose.'

'What is it Gnawberry?' asked Gnawra.

'We have to get these brave fellows across the river before nightfall.' Gnawberry plopped down into the water beside his wife. 'Just between you and me' he whispered to her, 'I don't fancy their chances but they have an important quest, a very important quest indeed, and you and I my dear, are going to help them. We can't risk carrying them across, the current is far too strong and I overheard them say they couldn't swim. Besides, they may be small but they're sturdy little fellows! No . . . there is only one thing for it. We'll have to build a dam. Let's get to work!'

The Beavers set too, chomping and chopping, gnawing and gnashing, pushing and pulling and heaving and hauling. They beavered away while Piper and Snoot stood anxiously by, watching and waiting. Just as the sun was beginning to immerse itself in the distant horizon, the busy Beavers jammed the last few branches into the dam. 'There, that should do it,' said Gnawberry. 'Well done old girl.'

'I don't know how to thank you,' said Piper to the Beavers as he and Snoot crossed safely to the other side of the river.

'You can thank us by coming back safe and sound,' said Gnawra.   Then Gnawberry suddenly remembered something.

'Hang on a tick!' he said and disappeared inside the Lodge. He emerged moments later carrying a short stick from which all the bark had been stripped away revealing the smooth whiteness beneath. 'Here, take Betula' he said, handing it to Piper. 'She's my lucky stick.'

'The stick is a *she* and *she* has a name?' exclaimed Snoot in surprise. Not being given to sentimentality he'd always preferred to call a stick, a stick.

'My mother always told me that Betula saved my life and somehow or other, in my mind she became *she*, and that's how I think of her, as *she*,' Gnawberry went on, disregarding Snoot's look of disbelief.

'She really saved your life? But how?' asked Piper, wondering how on earth a small white stick could save anybody's life.

'Well, I'll tell you,' said Gnawberry, settling himself comfortably on the river bank. 'When we were babies my brothers and sisters and I went down with a mysterious illness.'

Piper's heart sank as he realized that Gnawberry was about to embark on his life story, but he was far too polite to interrupt and so he let him go on.

'My mother tried all the usual things to make us better; berries, herbs, roots, that sort of thing, but nothing worked. Sadly, all of my brothers and sisters died. I was too young to remember but my mother told me that she was frantic with worry and desperate to save me. Every day she set out in search of a cure. The day my mother came home with Betula, I was barely holding on to life. Within an instant of nibbling on her bark, I was on the road to recovery. I've been as fit as a Flitterbug ever since. It was old Fusty the Badger who'd told her of a She Ferret who was an expert on plants and potions. My mother travelled all the way to the Forest of Mustela (a hostile, malodorous place, don't you know), to find the She Ferret and bring back the magic bark. So you see, Betula saved my life,' he said as he handed her to Piper. 'Who knows, even without her bark perhaps she'll bring you luck and keep you safe.'

'But she must be very precious to you. Won't you be needing her?' asked Piper.

'I have all the luck I could possibly want,' said Gnawberry grinning at Gnawra. 'Now you young fellows get on your way before it gets dark,' he said ushering them off. 'We'll keep the dam in good order until you get back. I hope you both find what you're looking for,' he added solemnly.

'Thank you Gnawberry, I promise to look after her,' Piper said as he tucked Betula safely into the thick fur behind his ear. *I'm going to need all the luck I can get*, he thought. 'This is it then, onwards and upwards.'

'It's now or never,' said Snoot as they looked back at their beloved Lumbery Wood.

It was dusk when the friends finally said their goodbyes to the Beavers and took the road that lead to the wide unknown. As the moon rose into the clear night sky Piper and Snoot reached the edge of the Bosky copse and the Wide River and the Lumbery Wood were left far

Four

Loupus and The Flornean Plain

As dawn crept onto the horizon Piper opened his eyes and tried to remember where he was. The musty scent of damp earth wafted on the cool morning air and brought him to his senses. Last night the mysterious nocturnal rustlings, the screeching of the owls, and the mournful howling of a wolf had permeated his dreams and it was a great relief to wake to the welcome light of day. Snoot was already up and making preparations for the journey. *He's relishing all this*, Piper thought a little enviously. *But I suppose it's no wonder, with Cracker and Stasha for parents. Adventure must run through his veins.*

'Time to make some plans,' said Snoot, 'now that you're awake, at last! We've a long journey ahead and the moon won't wait! May I borrow Betu'... your stick?' he asked, holding out his paw to Piper.

'You mean BETULA!' said Piper.

'If you insist,' said Snoot bowing with a flourish to Betula. He'd been busily clearing a patch of ground of its leaves and twigs and now he took the stick (rather roughly Piper thought) and drew the outlines of a map in the soft, moist earth.

'We are here,' he said, marking a cross to indicate their position. 'If I remember correctly what my parents taught me, we have to cross the Flornean Plain and head due south. If we cross here,' he said, jamming Betula into the ground, 'we might gain a day or two. It's the most

25

direct route but also the most hazardous. The safest way would be to take the pass across the Gorge of Gulch and follow the trail around the edge of the Tangly Wood . . . but no . . . that would take too long,' he reflected. 'No . . . I think it has to be this way!' Having now made up his mind, he dragged Betula through the dirt and jabbed her forcefully into the ground at every destination. 'We'll cross the Flornean Plain here . . . cut through the Forest of Mustela here . . . and approach Mount Florn from the Densim Pass around . . . here! That way our progress will go undetected by predatory eyes. Yep! That's our best bet,' he said with satisfaction as he handed a soil encrusted Betula back to Piper who was staring at his friend open mouthed in awe and admiration.

'Well, you're full of surprises! How on earth do you know all that stuff?'

'My parents of course,' said Snoot proudly. 'That is what nomads do!'

'But you never let on that you knew anything!' said Piper intrigued.

'I never expected to be going on a quest,' Snoot replied dismissively.

Piper was thoughtful as he cleaned Betula and tucked her back behind his ear. 'Do you know Snoot I know hardly anything about life outside the Lumbery Wood. Of course Pierre has told me stories, and Grandpa has often hinted at things.'

'Well, then this is your chance to find out,' said Snoot.

'The trouble is Snoot, I have the feeling I'd rather not know. I've already learned too much from Gnawberry.'

'You can't bury your head in your burrow forever Piper, you have responsibilities now,' Snoot said gently.

'You're right Snoot. The Spring Wake-up Song is my responsibility now and I'm determined not to let anybody down.' Then a worrying thought occurred to him. 'What if they come looking for us? With the dam in place they could easily cross the Wide River. Then there's Pierre! He would find us in no time! They'll try to stop us! I won't go home without my Voice Snoot! How long do you think we have before the moon is full?'

'It's hard to say,' said Snoot. 'A few more days perhaps. Long enough, if we don't waste time talking about it. We'll just have to get a move on and hope that we stay ahead of them.'

'Let's get going then,' said Piper urgently. He longed for them to come looking for him, just as much as he feared it but he couldn't risk having his resolve weakened.

As they took to the path a stealthy movement in the dense undergrowth ahead and the cracking and snapping of twigs, alerted them to the fact that they were not alone. Something large and heavy was prowling its way towards them. Piper's fur bristled.

'Don't move!' hissed Snoot. 'If we don't run it might leave us alone.'

'Are you sure?' squeaked Piper, who's first instinct was to run for his life. 'What in the world is it?'

'I don't know but it's not a mouse, that's for sure!' The two friends clung together, desperately trying to resist the temptation to run which might provoke the stalker to give chase.

After what seemed an age, the beast came to a halt just a hare's leap away from where they stood, helpless and afraid. It was too late to run now anyway. Then suddenly, out of the undergrowth burst a huge black wolf. He lunged onto the path barely a whisker away from the terrified pair and crouched motionless, head lowered, shoulders tensed, ready to pounce. Piper lost his head and snatched Betula from behind his ear, brandishing her in what he hoped was a menacing fashion. If ever he needed her luck, he needed it now! Then the wolf made his move.

'BOO!' he cried, springing towards them. The friends jumped back in shock and surprise and fell in a heap at the foot of the tree. 'HHAH!' cried the wolf delightedly. 'I make you jump, yes?' he inquired, tilting his head quizzically to one side. He was without doubt the handsomest wolf that ever was, and he regarded Piper and Snoot with a pair of the bluest eyes they'd ever seen. 'I make you jump, but I no frrrighten you?'

'A little,' lied Piper, who'd truly thought he was going to die. As the two friends picked themselves up and recovered their wits, the great black wolf sat down heavily on his haunches and uttered a long and pitiful sigh. Then shaking himself out of his reverie he grinned widely, flashing his sharp, white teeth.

'Ah well! It's good to hhave company. I am, hhow you say? Lone wolf. My pack they leave me hherrre alone to see if I can surrrvive. I no hhave stomich forrr thee hhont.'

The wolf had a way of rolling his r's and puffing out his h's which gave him a comical allure.

'Thee hhont?' inquired Piper looking at Snoot to see if he had understood.

'Yeh, you know, thee hhont; where you hhave to chase thee poorrr animal and kill hheem! I no can do! I am vegetarrrian wolf an' prrroud!' he said with a toss of his handsome head. 'My mutherrr, she come from Chowland, my fotherrr, hhe Nyetsky. Hhe pack leaderrr! Hhe want that one day I hhave pack of my own. They prrroud couple and I shame them forrr I no kill.'

'But how do you survive without meat?' asked Piper in surprise. 'I've never heard of a vegetarian wolf.'

'HHAH!' Exclaimed the wolf. 'I learrrn! At firrrst I verrry hhongrrry; nearrrly die! Then I discoverrr thee berrries, thee trrruffles, thee hherrrbs, and thee rrroots. Then I discoverrr thee cures, like yourrr stick,' he said nodding at Betula. 'She save life. I am in good shape no?' He turned elegantly, first one way then the other so that Piper and Snoot could appreciate the condition and beauty of his shiny black coat.

'Betula saved Gnawberry Beavers life, but how did you know?' asked Piper in amazement.

'It's like I say; I learrrn. Betula barrrk once save my life, but that is long storrry,' he said dismissively. 'My pack, when they come back forrr me, I surrrprrrise them! Make them prrroud! But hhow rrrude, I no intrrroduce! I am Loupus!' he said, bowing his head in greeting. 'And you arrre?'

'Piper Froom and Snoot Soozle, very pleased to meet you' said Piper.

'We're on a quest!' Snoot piped up.

'Quest? What is quest?' asked Loupus with a tilt of his head.

'We're on a quest to find Piper's Voice,' explained Snoot suddenly noticing that Piper was squirming with embarrassment. 'The problem is, he has to take over the Spring Wake-up Song but . . . well . . . he can't sing!'

Loupus sucked in his breath. 'Aaahhh . . . thee Sprrring Wake-up Song! I love thee Sprrring Wake-up Song! But I interrrupt! Please, go on.'

Snoot recounted Pierre's story, telling Loupus that they intended to rescue Piper's Voice from the Vishis Fween on the night of the full moon. Loupus listened silently and attentively until Snoot had finished speaking. 'Is verrry dangerrroos, thees quest! Tell me again. Why you need voice?' he said, turning to Piper who'd been hoping the ground would swallow him up and relieve him of his shame.

'Because Pa can't carry on, because the honour is now mine and because I'm the only Froom alive who can't sing,' mumbled Piper dejectedly. Then not wanting to be pitied by the big, black wolf, he shrugged his shoulders in a mock show of nonchalance. 'Pierre said, on the night of the full moon the Voices are left unguarded so we should be safe enough.' Speaking about the Voices suddenly reminded Piper of the urgency of his quest. 'We don't have much time though so if you'll excuse us, we must be off,' he said briskly.

'You no go alone! Is too dangerrroos. I go with you,' said Loupus. 'I know thee Florrrnean Plain, it can be trrreacherroos thees time of yearrr. I prrrotect you my frrriends!' he said proudly.

'Thank you Loupus, that would indeed be a privilege and a pleasure,' said Piper with gratitude. 'Onwards and upwards then!'

'It's now or never,' said Snoot.

And so it was that a Froom, a Soozle and a Wolf, set off together to cross the wind scoured and inhospitable Flornean Plain.

Five

In the Grip of the Eagle

The Flornean Plain stretched out like a gigantic carpet to the far horizon and rolled up its borders at the foot of Mount Florn. The terrain was rugged and bleak and the few scattered trees and scrubby bushes offered little shelter or protection from the harsh climate.

Piper and Snoot surveyed the vast, open emptiness with fear and trembling. This alien landscape with its boundless sky was a woodland creature's worst nightmare. They had only ever known the safe, dappled haven of the Lumbery Wood with its enveloping, protective canopy.

'Oh my twiskery tail! I never imagined it would be this . . . this . . . EXPOSED!' exclaimed Piper, staring around him in bewilderment. 'We can be seen by every raptor in the land!'

'And there's nowhere to hide!' gasped Snoot.

'Don't worrry my little frrriends, I am hhere to prrrotect you,' said Loupus reassuringly. 'I know thee Plain and all its perrrils. I was verrry frrrightened when my pack leave me hherrre,' he told them. 'I was young; no morrre than a pup, still wet behhind thee earrrs!'

'But how could they leave you in this place all alone?' asked Snoot aghast at the idea.

'My fotherrr, hhe think that if I am hhongry enough, I will hhave to hhont. Hhe was wrrrong! I no kill! I tell myself, if I can surrrvive hherrre in this desolate place, I can surrrvive anywherrre. And now my frrriends, I teach you everrrything I know!'

And so they began their long and arduous trek through the wilderness. Loupus showed them how he had learned to survive out there, all alone. His knowledge of plants was thorough and he taught them which were safe and good to eat and which were deadly poisonous. 'Just one little nibble on a moonseed drrrupe and you would die a hhorrrible, painful death!' Loupus warned them. 'Morrre than once I barrrely escape death thrrrough carrreless tasting.'

Piper was appalled! 'I was just about to eat one of those moonseeds,' he whispered to Snoot. 'They look so tempting!'

The wet, spring weather had provided an unexpected luxury for Snoot. 'Look over here,' he squealed excitedly. Beneath the moist rock that he'd just turned over lay a veritable larder of snails. Loupus and Piper watched in disgust as he cracked open one after the other and popped them into his mouth. 'Don't you want to try one?' he asked, in between mouthfuls. 'They're delicious. The best I've ever eaten!'

'I'll take your word for it thank you,' replied Piper, feeling rather queasy at the thought.

As the day wore on Piper and Snoot grew more accustomed to their strange surroundings and began to relax a little. Loupus had kept them entertained with stories which had made them laugh and cry.

'I hhave terrrible ache forrr my mutherrr and fotherrr and thee rrrest of thee pack,' he told them.

'I know what you mean,' said Snoot sadly and he told Loupus about how his parents had disappeared on the night of the Great Storm.

'Neverrr give up hope my frrriend,' said Loupus. 'I neverrr give up. I know my pack will come forrr me. Things hhave changed hherrre since they leave and I am afrrraid now to be alone.'

'You Loupus? What on earth do you have to be afraid of?' asked Piper in surprise. He thought him the strongest, bravest creature that ever lived.

'I hearrr things; strrrange sounds coming frrrom Mount Florrrn. I hhave bad feeling. In thee woods at night I see ominoos shadows everrrywherrre and I hhearrr pitiful crrries which strrrike terrror in my hhearrrt,' said Loupus fearfully. 'You should not go to Mount Florrrn,' he said to Piper, who was listening wide eyed with dismay at the thought of what might lie ahead of them. 'But I know you must,' Loupus added reluctantly. Snoot remained silent, his gaze fixed firmly on the ground in front of him and Piper knew that he was feeling guilty.

'The quest was my idea, remember?' he reassured him.

'But I did rather push you into it,' said Snoot sheepishly.

'Well we're here now so onwards and upwards,' said Piper more bravely than he felt and they continued their journey in thoughtful silence.

Throughout the day Piper had kept an eye on the vast open sky, half hoping, half dreading to see a large yellow Stonepecker pass overhead. He paused for a moment to rest and gazed up into the feathery clouds.

'Are you still looking for Pierre?' asked Snoot, breaking the silence.

'Yes,' replied Piper distractedly. 'I was sure he would have come looking for us by now.'

'Perhaps he doesn't know that we've gone,' said Snoot. 'You know how Pierre is; he's always going off to visit someone or other. Anyway, I thought you'd be relieved that they're not coming after us.'

'I am! I am relieved,' said Piper, but as the day wore on and there was no sign of Pierre, he began to feel abandoned. Why weren't they looking for him? Maybe, like Loupus' parents they thought he needed to learn. After all, a Froom who couldn't sing was of no use to anyone!

All day long the vultures had circled unremittingly overhead, watching and waiting. At first, Piper and Snoot had been terrified by their menacing presence. 'RAPTORS!' they had both screamed, clinging onto Loupus for dear life.

'You hhave nothing to fearrr frrrom thee bald guys,' he'd told them. 'They do verrry good clean-up job; eat only dead crrreaturrres.' They'd been horrified by how many carcasses they'd seen that day. Many of them had been there for a very long time and were nothing more than bleached bones but others were more recent and the flies swarmed over them in a rolling black cloud.

'I've never seen anything like this Snoot. Imagine how these poor creatures must have died out here all alone! If we didn't have Loupus' . . . Piper shuddered at the thought of their own bodies lying there smothered in flies, waiting to be picked clean by the Flornean caretakers. Snoot had fearfully examined all of the remains but Loupus had reassured him that there was not a single Soozle bone amongst them.

They had been walking now for the best part of a day and were in need of rest and shelter.

'We make good prrrogrrress my frrriends but now we must save ourrr strrrength forrr tomorrrow. Not farrr is trrrees and waterrr,' Loupus told them comfortingly. We rest there.

'I don't know about you Snoot but I can't wait to dip my aching paws into that cool water,' said Piper, relieved that their first day was almost over.

Suddenly, Loupus stopped dead in his tracks. A low, rumbling growl escaped from his throat and his shiny, black fur bristled as he sniffed the air. Piper was filled with a sense of fear and foreboding.

'What is it Loupus? What's wrong?'

The vultures, who had been following their progress all day had vanished from sight. A few wispy clouds trailed across the empty sky then without warning, a huge black shadow cast itself over the travellers and the whoosh, whoosh of a great bird's wings broke the quiet of the afternoon. Before they knew what was happening, Piper had been grasped in the vice-like grip of a huge pair of talons and swept up and away into the reddening sky. Within the blink of an eye he was nothing more than a speck in the distance. The last thing Piper heard was Loupus' anguished howl and Snoot's terrified scream. Then darkness closed in around him.

Six

Captured

Piper woke with a start as if from a nightmare. He felt that something terrible had happened to him; something that every small creature feared, and yet it seemed that he was still in one piece. He examined himself all over, just to be sure and although his head felt light and fuzzy and his sides ached, he was otherwise unharmed. *Oh my quivery withers! Where on earth am I and how did I get here?* The air was cold and thin and dried his sensitive nostrils which made him want to sneeze. With an effort he pulled himself up into a sitting position and looked around. He was surrounded by piles of sticks and grass which were roughly formed into a sort of basket. Overhead there was nothing but sky. Strange and frightening sounds came to his ears; sounds that he'd never heard before but which made his blood run cold. Then the horror of what had happened came flooding back to him. His aching sides reminded him of how he'd been gripped by those powerful talons and whisked into the air so fast that he couldn't breathe. He gasped at the realization. *Oh no! I think I'm dinner!*

Then the frightful whoosh, whoosh that he'd heard on the Plain moments before he was whisked away, announced the arrival of his fate. He cowered in fear for his life as two enormous birds alighted on the edge of what he now realized was their nest.

Piper's heart almost stopped beating.   He forced himself to look . . . up . . . and . . . up . . . and up, into two pairs of hungry eyes and two very sharp and ferocious looking beaks. Eagles! His worst fears were confirmed. Piper had never seen an eagle up close, but he'd seen them circling, high over Noggin Hill.   Pierre had told him that they were very fond of small furry creatures and to run for his life if one ever swooped. He shrank tremblingly into the bottom of the nest, closed his eyes and waited.

His short but happy life flashed before him in that moment that seemed to stretch into eternity.   When Grandma had gone to 'the beautiful sleep,' he had wondered what it would be like to die, but never in his wildest dreams had he imagined that it would happen in an eagles nest!

While Piper lay quivering, awaiting his untimely demise, Mrs Eagle spoke.   'Is that it?' she asked her husband in disgust.

'Is it not to your liking dear?' Mr Eagle replied.

'It's a Froom!' she exclaimed.   'One does not eat Froom! Don't you know that Frooms are lucky!'

Relief flooded over Piper and he opened his eyes in time to see Mr Eagle hang his noble head in shame.

'Don't you know that it's unlucky even to harm a Froom let alone to kill and eat one? Can't you do anything right?' she grumbled. Then Mr Eagle seemed suddenly to remember something.

'What about a Soozle? The Froom was with a Soozle. I could go back for it if you like dear?' *Oh No, not Snoot!* Piper almost shouted out loud.

'Soozle? Soozle? You expect me to eat Soozle? All I want is a tasty bit of meat! Is that too much to ask?'

Piper breathed again.   Even with Loupus there to protect him, Snoot wouldn't have stood a chance, and Mrs Eagle didn't mention anything about Soozles being lucky. His relief was immense but he was still very afraid.   *If they're not going to eat me, what are they going to do with me?   Perhaps they'll just throw me out!*   His already quivering body quivered a bit more at this horrible thought. *I have to escape!* he thought frantically.

While the Eagles were squabbling over what to have for dinner, he pulled himself up, slowly and gingerly so as not to attract their attention.   He found a small gap in the side of the nest and poked his paw into it until he'd made a hole big enough to peer through.   What he saw made him gasp in horror and fascination.   There spread out far, far below him lay the Flornean Plain.   To the West the mountains rose up vast and impregnable and to the East a vast, dense forest stretched as far as the eye could see. Directly beneath the nest, tall conifers climbed the mountainside, their sweeping branches draping the rocky outcrops like a giant, green blanket.   Piper couldn't believe his eyes.   He was almost at the top of Mount Florn and there on a plateau, on the side of the mountain, a seething mass of animals fought and wrangled amongst themselves. It was this, the unnatural cries and raucous chattering that had chilled Piper's blood.   The sight of the evil Fweens made his fur stand on end.   He'd never seen a Fween but he knew instinctively that this is what they were.   *If this is Mount Florn then I must be close to the Voices!* he thought. He pricked up his ears and listened but all he could hear was the squabbling of the Fween tribe and the continued hen pecking of Mrs Eagle.   There seemed to be no escape.

Piper sank back defeated into the bottom of the nest and stared up at the birds who were still arguing over the menu.

'Well, what can I get for you my dear?' Mr Eagle asked his wife, in an obvious effort to please her.

'Well, now that you ask, I was rather fancying a tender morsel of wild kitten,' she said dreamily. As she stared hungrily down at Piper he knew she was wishing that he were a wild kitten. Then she opened her beak and stretched menacingly towards him. He screwed up his eyes and rolled himself into a ball, hoping that the end would be quick. But it seemed that Mrs Eagle had other ideas. It was Betula that had caught her eye. She plucked the stick from behind Piper's ear and dropped it onto the rim of the nest. Piper's heart was already thumping like an alarmed jackrabbit but it beat a little faster when he saw Betula teetering on the edge. He didn't know whether to be relieved at not being eaten or frightened at the thought of losing Betula.

'How beautiful!' exclaimed Mrs Eagle. 'It's a *senshal!* It's exactly what I need for my nest-ormanent.' She picked up the smooth white stick and stuck it firmly into the rim of the nest. Her husband was looking at her quizzically and Piper could tell that he didn't have the faintest idea what she was talking about.

'Don't tell me you don't remember?' said Mrs Eagle, irritated by his puzzled expression. 'It was the old Chisel-beaked Stonepecker who told me that a nest-ormanent is a *senshul* in High Society.' She leaned back as far as she could without falling off the nest, closed one eye and surveyed her handy work. 'It was he who told me that Frooms are lucky. Don't you ever remember anything? The story of the Froom who burst the eardrums of a Vishis

Fween? He was a lucky Froom the Stonepecker said.' She sighed in exasperation at the stupidity of her gormless husband.

The old Chisel-beaked Stonepecker? She must mean Pierre. He's the only one that knows the story about Grandpa and the Vishis Fween, and everyone says he's a rare bird, Piper thought. The mention of Pierre suddenly brought his mind into focus. The idea that he might never see his home and family again, threw him into a panic. Here he was, trapped in an eagle's nest, probably about to die and SHE had stolen Betula. The altitude was beginning to make him light headed and before he knew what he was doing, he had blurted it out!

'NO! You can't have her! She's my lucky stick!' he shouted. Mrs Eagle looked scornfully down her beak at Piper before turning back to her husband.

'What do you think dear?' she said.

'I think he's a very plucky little fellow,' said Mr Eagle admiringly.

'Not the Froom! The *senshal*!' she exclaimed as she moved the stick a little closer to the outer edge of the nest where it could be more readily appreciated by the rest of the High Society.

'There! That's perfect!' she said with satisfaction. Piper could see her husband visibly begin to relax. He was obviously thinking that at least he'd done something right. Then she turned her sharp beady eyes upon him and glared at him contemptuously.

'I'm still hungry!' she snapped peevishly. 'And what pray tell, are we going to do with this?' The Eagles peered down at Piper who, dismayed by his sudden outburst, was attempting to make himself invisible in the bottom of the nest.

'I think I should take him back to his friends,' said Mr Eagle who seemed to have developed quite a soft spot for Piper.

'You'll do nothing of the sort!' retorted Mrs Eagle. 'I'm hungry and I need you to find me something tasty and nourishing to eat. I don't know how you expect me to lay eggs, rear a family and run a nest on nothing more than an inedible Froom.'

'But what are we going to do with him?' said Mr Eagle staring down at Piper.

'Don't you worry about the Froom, I'll dispose of him. You just concentrate on getting me something to eat.'

'Very well dear,' said Mr Eagle with a heartfelt sigh. He glanced once more at Piper, shook his head sadly, and took off with a whoosh over the mountains.

Piper now found himself at the mercy of Mrs Eagle and relief turned to fear once again. *Oh my shivering whiskers! Whatever am I going to do?* he thought frantically. Mrs Eagle had turned her attention back to Betula and for the moment was preoccupied with arranging and rearranging her. She turned the stick this way and that, cocking her head to one side and squinting to take in the full effect of the beautiful object. 'They'll be so jealous when they see my beautiful *senshal* nest-ormanent! I'll be the envy of all the High Society!' she said to no one in-particular.

Piper saw his chance. *I have to get out of here! I'm not going to wait around to find out how she intends to dispose of me!* While Mrs Eagle's back was turned he scrambled hurriedly onto the rim of the nest and stood trembling and teetering on its edge. Perched high up there on the side of Mount Florn, he had only one choice. He had to jump. As he looked down on the vertiginous drop to the trees below his stomach churned and his head span. He remained there, teetering indecisively until Mrs Eagle looked up from her titivating. 'There! Now for the Froom!' she said purposefully.

Piper closed his eyes and leaped for his life.

Seven

Grizel to the Rescue

The blanket of trees that had seemed so far away, came up to meet him at breakneck speed. He hit the first branch which knocked the wind out of him but caught him like a hammock. It strained under his weight, then flexed its limb and tossed him violently onto the branch below. Piper was flung ferociously from branch to branch and from tree to tree, bouncing first on his head, then his feet, then on his back, then his front until he had somersaulted halfway down the mountainside. He arrived with a heavy thud on the forest floor where he lay battered, bruised and bewildered. *I wonder if I'm still alive?* he thought hazily. As he lay trying to figure it out, the ground under him started to heave and roll and he thought that perhaps he was dead after all and the earth was about to swallow him up. He tried to get to his feet but his head was still whirling from his chaotic descent. Then the writhing mass beneath him suddenly rose up and let out a shrill cry.

'Gerroff me you great galumphing buffoon!' it shrieked.

Piper was tossed aside as a woolly creature jumped to its feet and shook the long hair from out of its eyes. It stared angrily at him through its thick, unruly fringe of red hair.

'You can't just go landing on innocent creatures without a by-your-leave!' Cursing and muttering it shook itself and checked itself over for broken bones. When it was satisfied there was no damage done, it addressed Piper once more. 'Where did you come from anyway?' it said, eyeing him up suspiciously.

Piper was still reeling from the ordeal of his kidnap and his headlong descent through the trees, and felt incapable of a sensible explanation. 'Up there,' he said pointing to the sky. 'Eagles nest.'

'What are you, some kind of adrenalin freak?' it shrieked, aghast.

'I'm a Froom!' he said, indignant that this irate, woolly creature should be shrieking so rudely at him after what he'd just been through. 'Piper Froom if you must know, and who and what might you be?'

'Ooohh, touchy aren't we? I'm a squirrel actually, and my friends call me Grizel.'

'Grizel by name and Grizel by nature,' retorted Piper. Having survived the Eagles and his fall, he was beginning to feel rather brave.

'Well, if you're a Froom, prove it! Sing something!'

Piper glared at her for a moment in silence, searching his mind for a way out of his embarrassing predicament. He didn't want to admit to this feisty, hairy creature that he was the only Froom alive who couldn't sing.

'Well?' she persisted.

Piper gave up. 'Can't sing,' he mumbled hanging his head in shame.

'I'm sorry. Did I hear you say you can't sing? You've got to be kidding! A Froom that can't sing!' she shrieked delightedly. 'It's not every day that a Froom drops out of the sky, but one that can't sing! That's awesome!' Grizel seemed to have shaken off her grumpiness and was now jumping up and down and chortling with glee.

'I don't see what's so funny,' said Piper miserably. 'If I don't find my Voice there won't be any more Spring Wake-up Song and creatures could die because of me!'

Grizel suddenly stopped her bouncing and chortling and stared at him in horror.

'What do you mean, if you don't find your Voice?'

'That's what I came here to do. I'm going to Mount Florn to rescue my Voice from the Vishis Fween. It's waiting for me right now,' said Piper as convincingly as he could.

'Are you crazy! Have you completely lost your marbles! No one comes back from Mount Florn! The Fweens are everywhere, you don't stand a chance. All the creatures round here live in fear of those evil beasts and now you're telling me that you're going to Mount Florn . . . AND . . . that there is to be no more Spring Wake-up Song! We're all doomed!'

Grizel's body slumped in an attitude of misery. Her long, woolly fringe hung down from her drooping head and covered her eyes. Then just as quickly, she recovered herself, threw back her hair and shrieked; 'what are you going to do about it then? We all depend upon the Spring Wake-up Song! You have to find your Voice, you have to find it!'

'And that's exactly what I intend to do but first I have to get back to my friends, Snoot and Loupus who probably think that I'm already dead, then I have to get . . . up there, (he was unwilling to say the dreaded words for fear of upsetting her again), on the night of the full moon and rescue my Voice and . . . well . . . that's really all there is to it,' Piper said, shrugging his shoulders.

'Where are they now, these friends of yours?' inquired Grizel ignoring his pretended indifference.

'Somewhere out there on the Flornean Plain,' said Piper defeatedly. 'How am I ever going to find them now?'

'Don't you worry about that my little Froomy friend,' chirped Grizel. 'I can see everything from up there,' she said looking up into the tall trees. 'If your friends are out there I'll find them. I've got eyes like a Hawk!'

Piper flinched at the very mention of the word but before he could respond, she was already up and away into the topmost branches. A moment later she was back. He felt exhausted just watching her whirlwind activities.

'They're still out there but they're a very long way off,' she said. 'At least half a days march I'd say.'

'Half a day! But I haven't got half a day! And it'll be dark soon! And to think that I was so close to my Voice up there on Mount Florn and now it could be lost to me forever. Oh what's the use!' he cried, as he sank dejectedly to the ground.

Grizel glared incredulously at him through her fringe. 'What a quitter! Your Voice is up there waiting for you, your friends are out there waiting for you and all you can do is sit there and snivel!'

'Do you have any better ideas?' said Piper wearily.

'As a matter of fact I do,' said Grizel. 'I'll fly you there myself!'

'I suppose you think that's funny too,' Piper retorted.

Grizel bounced up and down shrieking with glee, then she stood in front of him and spread out her limbs unfolding her bat like wings. She performed a graceful pirouette to show off her woolly cape. Piper stared open mouthed, speechless with wonder.

'You can really fly?'

'Well, why else would I have wings?' she snapped impatiently. 'Now, are you going to sit there sulking all day or shall we go and find your friends?' Piper leaped to his feet.

'Perhaps I am a lucky Froom after all,' he said happily.

'You'll have to climb the tree first. I'll never get off the ground with a lump like you on my back!' said Grizel. Piper looked up at the tall fir which towered above him. He'd never climbed a tree before but then again, he was doing lots of things he'd never done before. He spat on his paws and began to climb. The branches were a long way apart and there wasn't much to get a grip on but Grizel bounced up and down around him, hauling and tugging him from above, then pushing and shoving him from below until eventually, breathless and exhausted they reached the topmost branches. Far away in the distance, Piper could just make out the tiny forms of his friends. Nothing else moved on the Flornean Plain except the shadows of the Vultures who'd resumed their ariel patrol.

'Climb aboard and hold on tight,' said Grizel after a moments rest. Piper climbed onto her back and held on for dear life. 'Try not to strangle me!' she shrieked. Then she opened her woolly cape and leaped off into space. They sped through the air and over the treetops so fast that Piper could hardly catch his breath. He gasped and spluttered and his eyes streamed as the cold air rushed past. Grizel whooped and shrieked with the sheer joy of flying and Piper began to enjoy himself. The world looked so small and benign from above. The Flornean Plain which had so terrified him from the ground, looked serene and unthreatening from on high. Grizel flew like the wind and Piper, hanging onto her woolly mane, wished that he could stay up there forever. He never wanted it to end. But the tiny figures of his friends grew rapidly larger and he was eager to be reunited with them. They were so close now that he could see their expressions of amazement as they gawped, open mouthed at the spectacle. Then suddenly, Grizel veered sharply away and headed back to the forest.

'What are you doing?' Piper yelled in her ear.

'We're too late Piper, that wolf's got your friend,' Grizel shouted over her shoulder.

'That wolf *is* my friend. Turn around, it's all right. Really!'

After a moments hesitation, Grizel circled back around and came in to land a good distance away from where Loupus and Snoot were staring in wonderment. Piper leaped off her back and ran full pelt to his surprised friends. Their joy at his return was almost overwhelming. 'Oh Piper, we thought we'd never see you again! Are you all right?' cried Snoot jumping on his friend and almost knocking him over. 'How on earth did you manage to escape from the eagle?'

'Eagles!' said Piper. 'There are two of them, Mr and Mrs and apparently, I'm lucky! Mrs Eagle said so, although I don't think it would have stopped her from eating me if she'd liked the look of me. I was meant to be dinner!'

Piper quickly filled them in on how he'd woken to find himself in the Eagles nest on the side of Mount Florn. 'And Mrs Eagle stole Betula, and then I jumped from the nest while her back was turned!'

'You jumped!' gasped Loupus in amazement. 'You must be verrry lucky Frrroom to surrrvive a jump like that!'

'I am,' said Piper, 'but the luckiest thing that happened to me was finding Grizel.' He prudently decided not to say any more about what he'd seen from the Eagles nest. He didn't want to frighten Snoot and he was sure that Loupus would try to prevent them from going on with the quest if he knew just how many Fweens were up there on Mount Florn.

Grizel had been keeping an eye on Loupus and was nervously moving in closer, until she was satisfied that he posed no threat. Reassured by the way he'd greeted Piper, she now bounced confidently into their midst. 'He didn't exactly find me,' she said. 'He knocked me rudely from my bed then tried to suffocate me! I was in the middle of my afternoon nap when he dropped in on me unannounced,' she told Snoot and Loupus, by way of introduction.

'Snoot, Loupus . . . meet my friend Grizel,' Piper said laughing. 'She's amazing! A flying squirrel! Who'd have thought!'

'And a Froom who can't sing! Who'd have thought!' she teased, trying to hide her discomfiture at his praise. 'But what's all this about Betula? Who is she and where is she now?' she said, quickly changing the subject.

'It's a stick and it's a she,' Snoot piped up, 'and she saved Gnawberry Beaver's life! Piper sets great store by her. He thinks that she might save his life too.'

Piper was wriggling with embarrassment and willing Snoot to shut up. He knew that Grizel would think it ridiculous that he could be so attached to a stick! He was thankful when Loupus came to his rescue. 'Piperrr, hhe keep Betula safe forrr Gnawberry. Hhe think, one day perrrhhaps, she may hhelp hhim too.'

'But now Mrs Eagle has her as a *senshal* nest-ormanent so I'll just have to get used to it,' Piper said, trying to sound unconcerned.

'You really believe that a stick could save your life?' Grizel said shrieking with laughter.

'I don't see why not, she saved Gnawberry's!' snapped Piper defensively. He wasn't usually given to snapping but Grizel brought out a side of him he didn't know he had.

'Piper is on a very important quest to find his Voice and he needs all the help he can get!' Snoot said indignantly. Only he was allowed to poke fun at Piper. Grizel suddenly stopped laughing and fell into silent reflection.

'Don't you worry, my Froomy friend,' she said after a moments contemplation. 'If Betula really means that much to you, I'll get her back for you. I'm not frightened of that stuck up old bird!'

'No! No! Piper yelled. 'She'll kill you!'

'I can't stand here chewing the fat all day long! Right now this flying squirrel has to fly,' she called over her shoulder. Grizel had already set off at a run and was now taking a flying leap into the air. She soared straight up like a kite on the wind, then circled momentarily over their heads before heading off back to the forest of tall firs that climbed the side of Mount Florn.

Piper called after her until her diminishing form merged with the dark background of the trees and disappeared from view. 'Oh what have I done?' he wailed. 'Mrs Eagle will have for her dinner! I don't want Betula!

It's just a stupid stick!' Piper was inconsolable. He liked his feisty new friend and now he had put her in terrible danger.

'Come! We must rrrest, it is late,' said Loupus taking control of the situation. 'I think yourrr frrriend Grrrizel can take carrre of hherrrself,' he said gently to Piper.

By the time they'd reached the shelter of the trees under which they would spend the night, Piper's spirits had recovered a little. *Loupus is right,* he thought. *Grizel is far too clever to do anything stupid. She wouldn't risk her life for a stick! Would she?* Then he quickly put the thought out of his mind. *I can do something for her though! I can find my Voice! I WILL find my Voice!*

Piper's head was buzzing with the days events and with his new friend, Grizel. He had quite forgotten that Snoot was still quietly looking for his parents and that Loupus still yearned to be reunited with his pack.

It was dark when they finally settled themselves down and the night was bright and cold. Loupus sat a little way off staring into the distance and sniffing the air, then he lifted his head to the rising moon and howled a long and haunting howl. From far away in the West came an answering howl, followed swiftly by another, and then another until they all became one and the night was filled with the spine tingling sound. Piper and Snoot had already drifted off into an exhausted sleep and were oblivious to this momentous event. They were unaware that Loupus had been so overcome with emotion that a large tear had rolled down his handsome nose and plopped into the dust at his feet.

That night as the howling of the wolves filtered through his slumbers, Piper dreamed that he was flying on the wings of a song. A song so beautiful and haunting that it filled the skies with its soaring notes and reached to the four corners of the land. In his dream all who heard it were spellbound and he knew that he had found his Voice at last.

Eight

The Proclamation of the Vishis Fween

Since the departure of the wolves (who they feared beyond reason) the Fweens had been returning to Mount Florn in their droves. They were voracious killers and it wasn't long before they'd hunted, almost to extinction, the creatures that had once inhabited the mountain. With their convenient larder severely depleted they had grown quarrelsome and unruly. In a bid to maintain control of the rabble, their tyrannical leader, the Vishis Fween, had been forced to impose a new regime upon his tribe. Summoning them to the plateau he had made his proclamation.

'I DECREE THAT THERE IS TO BE NO MORE KILLING!' he had announced to the assembled horde. The Fweens had gone berserk, baying and screaming in rage and the Vishis Fween had been in danger of being torn to pieces by his own tribe.

'UNTIL THE NIGHT OF THE FULL MOON!' he'd roared over the din. The tribe had quietened down, intrigued by what might follow.

'ON THE NIGHT OF EVERY FULL MOON THERE IS TO BE A GREAT CHASE! There'd followed an expectant hush while their leader glared menacingly around at the tribe. After savouring a moment of complete control he'd continued. 'YOU WILL ALL FEAST AND

GORGE TO YOUR HEART'S CONTENT!' This was more like it! They'd whooped and screamed with jubilation at the excellence of this new regime.

'SILENCE!' They'd known there would be a price to pay and now the hubbub subsided into mutterings of suspicion.

'UNTIL THAT NIGHT YOU WILL LIVE ONLY ON SLUGS AND SNAILS! YOU WILL HONE YOUR APPETITES FOR THE GREAT CHASE! IF ANYONE DARES TO DISOBEY ME . . .' he'd glared fiercely around at the bewildered Fweens, daring any of them to challenge him. It was the delicious idea of a night of chasing and gorging that had finally won them over. They'd felt the sacrifice was worth it, after all slugs and snails weren't so bad. They'd bowed willingly to the wisdom of their powerful leader and become compliant and respectful.

From that day on they'd begun to hunt far and wide. The prospect of the Great Chase and a consuming, gnawing hunger drove them on, compelling them to widen their territory in search of more exotic fare. Their fear of wolves kept them away from the Flornean Plain, even after the pack's departure, but they roamed large areas of forest and woodland striking terror into the hearts of defenseless creatures. No one was safe. With the wolves gone the Fweens feared nothing. There was a story that had once made their blood curdle but that was now a dim, distant memory. Legend had it that an entire Fween tribe had been overthrown by a singing Froom who'd exploded the eardrums of the Vishis Fween, with his piercing voice. But time had added incredulity to its telling and many of them believed that no such creature ever existed. It was often jeeringly referred to as 'The Scary Froom Myth.'

The Fweens were cowardly. They would kidnap their poor unsuspecting victims from their dens and burrows in the dead of night and drag the terrified and bewildered creatures up the steep mountain pass of Mount Florn to the cave of the Vishis Fween. Here they were imprisoned and guarded day and night by their leader. He alone was exempt from the decree but modestly took only the smallest (and tenderest) of the captives, to sustain him throughout the month.

Escape was impossible for the stricken prisoners. There were many who had tried but no creature had ever come back from Mount Florn. The villainous Fweens took great delight in the snatching of their prey but the real sport had not yet begun.

On the night of the Great Chase the beasts, now demented with hunger, would assemble on the plateau and voraciously await the conveyance of the prisoners. Their leader would prove his supreme authority by biding his time, prolonging the moment while the tribe bayed and screamed for blood. Only when the full moon had reached its zenith and the Fweens were at fever pitch would the Vishis Fween begin the festivities. He would herd the terrified prisoners onto the plateau, take his place in the centre and proclaim in a thundering roar;

'LET THE GREAT CHASE BEGIN!'

What followed is too awful and gruesome to recount but the next day the Fween tribe would be satisfied, docile and obedient and for many days to come the vultures would feast at will. The Vishis Fween had demonstrated his power and supremacy over his tribe.

Had Pierre known the true horror of what took place every full moon night, he wouldn't have told Piper his story of the enchanting Voices.

Had Piper understood what he'd seen from the Eagles nest he would have turned tail and fled for home.

The night of the full moon was approaching. On the plateau of Mount Florn the Fweens, now half crazed with hunger and expectation were gathering in their hordes and the cave of the Vishis Fween was filled with terrified creatures awaiting their horrible fate.

Nine

The Return of the Pack

The sun had not even nudged its way past the horizon when Piper was awakened by a gentle but insistent prodding. His wonderful dream was still tugging him back into sleep and it took a great effort of will to rouse himself. During the night Loupus had been restless and fidgety and Piper had been woken several times by the rumble of a deep and shuddering sigh. It came back to him now as he watched Loupus pace anxiously up and down. Beside him, Snoot stretched and yawned.

'Is it morning already?' he mumbled sleepily.

'Only just,' replied Piper, 'but I think Loupus has been awake for a while. He was very restless last night.'

'Come! Rrrattle yourrr lazy bones!' said Loupus, now that they were both awake. 'The day is alrrready hhalf overrr! If we leave now, we could rrreach the Forrrest of Mustela by nightfall.'

Piper got up and rubbed his eyes. The events of yesterday seemed like a distant dream, but Grizel came insistently to the forefront of his mind. He hoped with all his heart that she wouldn't act upon her words. 'Do you think she'll try to find Betula, Snoot?'

'There's no time to worry about Betula or Grizel,' Snoot replied. 'Loupus is getting twitchy.'

'Come, my frrriends! We must hhurry!' he called as he paced the ground impatiently. 'We hhave a long jourrrney ahhead and verrry little time. The moon will soon be full.'

'He's right Snoot, we only have one chance. We have to be there when the Voices are unguarded or all will be lost. We can't risk an encounter with the Fweens. The very thought of it makes my fur stand on end.'

'We'd better get a move on then,' said Snoot.

They set off at a trot but with Loupus' loping stride he was soon well ahead of them. They tried to keep up but their Guardian seemed oblivious to his two small charges and by midday they lagged far behind. They were exhausted, hungry and thirsty having barely had time to nibble on a cush cush root and sip from the stream, before setting out. All through the long morning's trek, Piper had scanned the skies, in the hopes of catching a glimpse of Grizel. He'd long since given up looking for Pierre having decided that he and Snoot had been abandoned to their fate.

'You're worried . . . about Grizel . . . aren't you Piper,' said Snoot breathlessly. 'She doesn't . . . strike me as . . . the sort of squirrel that . . . would do anything stupid.'

'I know . . . but I can't . . . stop . . . worrying . . . about her,' puffed Piper as he slogged along beside Snoot. 'It's no use Snoot . . . can't carry on.'

'Me . . . neither. Have to . . . rest.' They stopped to catch their breaths. Loupus was now so far ahead that they were in danger of losing him completely.

'LOUPUS! LOUPUS!' they called with what little breath they had left. Loupus turned around in surprise. It was as if he'd forgotten their very existence.

'My poorrr frrriends. Hhow inconsiderrrate of me!' he exclaimed as he arrived back at their sides. 'I hhave worrrn you out! What am I thinking! We must stop and rrrest!'

Piper and Snoot flopped thankfully onto the rough, stony ground while Loupus continued to pace distractedly. 'He's behaving very strangely,' said Snoot when he'd recovered his breath. 'Do you think there's something wrong with him?'

'I don't know,' said Piper with concern. 'He did a lot of sighing last night.' As he watched Loupus circling the ground, the truth suddenly hit him. 'It's his pack!' he exclaimed. 'They've come back for him! Oh what an idiot I am Snoot! If I hadn't been so preoccupied with my own selfish thoughts, I would have realized earlier. I heard them calling to him in the night but I thought it was just a dream. He's leaving them behind so that he can take care of us!'

'But he's waited all his life for this moment!' said Snoot in dismay. 'He has to go back. We must carry on without him.'

'You're right!' agreed Piper. 'It can't be more than half a day's trek to the Forest of Mustela. I think we can make it by ourselves; but it won't be easy getting Loupus to change his mind. He feels responsible for us.'

It was just as Piper had predicted. Loupus confirmed that his pack had returned and that they'd called to him in the night. 'But I no leave my frrriends! I make prrromise,' he'd said proudly. 'I wolf who keep worrrd.'

'But you must go to your pack. They're calling to you and you've waited so long for them,' Piper insisted.

'And you've taught us everything we need to know. We'll be fine Loupus, really!' Snoot affirmed.

Eventually, after much argument Loupus relented but he wouldn't leave until he was satisfied they could truly manage without him. He went over everything he'd taught them, testing them, asking them questions, then when he was satisfied that they'd answered everything correctly, he reluctantly conceded that they were ready to go it alone.

'You hhave learrrned well my frrriends; and now you must go to yourrr quest and I must go to my pack,' he said, his voice breaking with emotion. Then he turned to Snoot. 'Don't lose hhope,' he told him. 'What good is a life without hhope, hhuh?' Snoot blinked back a tear. 'You my frrriend,' he said to Piper. 'I know you will find yourrr Voice. You arrre one verrry deterrrmined and one verrry lucky Frrroom!' Piper swallowed hard in an effort to keep his composure. He had to let Loupus think that they were up to the challenge of taking care of themselves even if he wasn't quite so confident himself.

Finally and reluctantly they said their goodbyes and with a wave of his tail and his head held high, Loupus loped briskly off in the direction from which they had just come. The two friends stood silently watching as their trusty friend and Guardian went to meet his long-lost pack.

'Well, Snoot, it's just you and me again,' said Piper as he scanned the skies in the vain hope of seeing Grizel. There, way up on high an eagle was circling and Piper's courage began to ebb. 'Let's get out of here before it comes back,' he said nodding towards the bird which was thankfully, little more than a speck in the distance.

Once again they set off at a trot, anxious to reach the safety of the forest before nightfall. The comforting thought of shady trees and green shoots spurred them on and kept them focused. To Piper's great consternation the Eagle stayed with them but he remained on high, soaring on the thermals. The terrain was becoming increasingly rugged, forcing them to slacken their pace. After several hours of clambering up and down the rocky slopes and slipping and sliding on the loose scree, they were weary and footsore.

'Ooch! ouch! My paws are not made for this hard, stony ground,' squealed Piper.

'It can't be far now,' puffed Snoot. 'The sun's already low.' Snoot had been looking up at the sky as he spoke and hadn't seen the large boulder that lay in his path. He tripped and fell, tumbling head over heals down the steep incline into a deep crevice where he lay motionless.

'Snoot, Snoot, are you all right?' Piper called to him. Snoot didn't move. Piper couldn't see him clearly from where he stood but someone had a birds eye view. He looked up fearfully, in time to see the Eagle fold its wings and drop like a stone out of the sky. It was heading straight for Snoot.

'Snoot! Snoot!' Piper screamed. Snoot remained motionless as the eagle swooped in, grabbed it's quarry and whooshed off with a flap of it's great wings. Piper watched in disbelief as Mr Eagle circled overhead, the limp, lifeless form dangling helplessly from his talons. Then he flew off back towards Mount Florn with his catch. Piper stared down into the crevice.

'Snoot!' he screamed.

'I'm all right Piper,' said Snoot picking himself up and scrambling back up the slope.

'Oh Snoot, I thought you were a gonner! I thought Mr Eagle was after you!' cried Piper

'He saved my life Piper! The reason I couldn't move or call out was that I was nose to nose with a rattlesnake! Mr Eagle's huge talons almost ripped my ear off as he snatched it away from me!'

'So all that time he was protecting us? Watching over us?' said Piper incredulously.

'It seems so, and I for one am very glad of his presence. I would have been a gonner if he hadn't been there.'

'Well I guess I must have made quite an impression upon him,' said Piper proudly.

'And don't forget that you're lucky,' said Snoot.

'I think you're pretty lucky too,' Piper laughed, 'but now, if you don't have any broken bones, we'd better get going. It's too nerve wracking out here in the open, we need to get back in the woods. Imagine Snoot, green shoots, cool, fresh air and the dappled sunlight filtering through the whispery leaves. Aahhh! I can hardly wait.'

'Well, if you put it like that! Onwards and upwards!' said Snoot.

The light was beginning to fade when the weary travellers finally reached the borders of the Plain and descended into the lush green valley. There spread out beneath them like a fathomless sea lay a vast, dense forest.

'Oh my sniffly snout! Look how dark it is Snoot!' said Piper, his heart heavy with disappointment. 'I imagined it would be more like the Lumbery Wood, safe and welcoming and . . . and . . . well, anything but this gloomy blackness.'

'It looks so forbidding and hostile,' gasped Snoot.

They stood and stared in silent trepidation at the bleak forest that stretched as far as the eye could see.

'Well, we can't stay out here in the open tonight without any protection. We'll be safer under cover of the forest,' Piper said, doubting even his own words.

'Without Loupus to protect us we're sitting ducks out here,' said Snoot nodding in agreement.

As the night closed in the two friends plucked up their courage and prepared to enter the sinister, brooding darkness of the Forest of Mustela.

Ten

The Dark Forest of Mustela

A strong, acrid odour hung in the air and brought tears to the eyes of the two travellers. Piper remembered what Loupus had said about dark shadows and screams in the night and a shiver ran down his spine. 'I don't like this place Snoot, it scares me,' he said as they prepared to face their first night alone in the forbidding Forest.

'It scares me too,' replied Snoot with a shudder.

The forest was alive with furtive rootings, rustlings, scratchings and scrapings and they jumped with fright at every unfamiliar sound. It was as black as pitch under the tangled branches and they had to employ all their senses as they searched for a hole or a hollow in which to spend the night.

'Stay close Snoot, I don't want to lose you in the dark,' whispered Piper.

'Don't worry, I'm right behind you! SSsshhhh! What's that? There's something out there Piper and that smell's getting stronger!'

'Now I'm really scared!' Piper hissed.

Just then, the moon which had been making its steady ascent through the night sky, cleared the treetops and a silvery light poured down onto a small clearing. Piper and Snoot stood rooted in horror as they found themselves surrounded by a motley clan of fearsome looking ferrets.

'Oh Snoot!' hissed Piper. 'Remember what Gnawberry said?' You wouldn't want to find yourselves in a ferret camp!'

'Well, well, well! Lookee 'ere boys!' said a disembodied voice. There was a scrambling in the undergrowth as a large, brawny ferret bounced his way over to where Piper and Snoot stood trembling with fear. He skipped around them, hungrily eyeing them up and down, sniffing them from head to toe, then he poked a bony paw into Piper's plump side. 'We'll eat well tonight boys; rich pickin's indeed and easy got!'

The rest of the Ferret clan moved in for a closer inspection of the intruders and for their share of the prodding, poking and sniffing. 'What yer doin' 'ere on our stompin' ground?' demanded the Chief Ferret, as he shoved the clan roughly back into line. Piper and Snoot were too afraid to speak and clung mutely together. 'Aahh, look at that boys, ain't it touchin.' Them's proper little babes in the wood!' The clan found this remark very amusing and laughed and danced around the frightened pair chanting, *babes in the wood! Babes in the wood!* until the Chief Ferret called them to order.

'That's enough now boys, show a bit o' respect for the babes. Now then, where were we? Oh yeh. What yer doin' ere in my camp?' he barked in Piper's face.

'We're on our way to Mount Florn on a quest to find Piper's Voice,' squeaked Snoot in a panic.

'And what's Piper when 'ees at 'ome?' barked the Chief Ferret, turning his attention to Snoot.

'He's a Froom,' mumbled Snoot, wishing that he'd kept his mouth shut.

'A Froom! Is 'ee indeed?' said the Chief Ferret taking a step backwards. The story of the Froom who burst the eardrums of a Vishis Fween was legendary and the Chief Ferret wasn't taking any chances. 'Back off boys, give the little fella's some space,' he said with a new found respect. Then he crept in a little closer and gave Piper one more tentative sniff. 'So what's this Voice yer lookin' for?' he demanded inquisitively. Piper mustered all his courage and forced himself to speak up.

'Well, you see,' he mumbled, 'I can't sing so I have to go to Mount Florn to find my Voice because next spring it will be my turn to sing the Spring Wake-up Song and . . . '

'The Spring Wake-up Song!' exclaimed the Chief Ferret with a sharp intake of breath. These words seemed to have an extraordinary effect on him. He sank back on his haunches, his eyes wide with wonder, then very softly, almost to himself, he began to sing;

Spring is here
Spring is cheer
Twisker your whiskers
Untangle your hair

At this point in the song, the rest of the Ferret clan joined in;

Frisker your tails and twingle your toes
Come out and sniff the new blown rose
Wake up, get up for Spring has sprung
Trimble your trotters, come join the song
Patter your paws, come sing along

For Spring is now and Spring is cheer

Spring is . $h^{ee}eee^*_eee^*e_e^*eer^*r^re^{**}$!

The rendition ended with the last high note fizzing off in all directions and the result was rather alarming. Piper and Snoot looked at each other in bewilderment. Piper didn't know whether to laugh or cry. One minute he'd thought they were going to die and the next, the Ferrets were singing (or rather caterwauling) the Spring Wake-up Song!

The Chief Ferret jumped to his feet and wiped a tear from his eye. 'Don't worry, we ain'tgonnuwurtyer,' he said.

'What did he say?' Snoot whispered.

'I think he said they aren't going to hurt us,' Piper whispered back.

'I'm Froshus,' said the Chief Ferret, stepping forward and introducing himself, and them lot there's . . . and he proceeded to introduce all twenty five of the Ferrets, one by one. . . Abe, Biggins, Chomper, Dimly, Eavel, Gnasher, Hopper, Iggy, Jaws, Kosher, Legs, Muggins, Nasty' . . . 'And this last one 'ere is Zoot-Alors. His mother was French,' Froshus added in a whisper.

'Enchanté' said a beaming Zoot-Alors with a theatrical bow and a flourish of his paw.

'Likewise,' said Piper bowing in response. 'I'm Piper Froom and this is my friend Snoot Soozle.'

'Escargot!' said Snoot bowing and showing off with the only French word he knew.

The introductions over, Froshus shooed the unruly ferrets back into a semblance of order before turning to Piper.

'It melts me 'art, the Spring Wake-up Song,' he said dreamily. It brings the forest alive and keeps life reg'lar. Balance! that's what me old Ma used to say when I was a nipper, always askin' questions. Froshus, she'd say, there 'as to be balance. Without balance there ain't no meanin.' Whenever I 'ear the song and see all the creatures comin' ter life, it makes sense of 'er words.'

'Can you hear it from here?' Piper asked, feeling a bit more at ease at finding that Gnawberry had got it wrong and the Ferrets weren't sneaky little blighters after all.

'Oh yeh,' said Froshus. 'If the wind's in the right direction, but usually we go to the northern borders for the Spring Ekwynox to celybrate with our cousins, the Weasels. We 'ere it plain as day from there. Me old dad used to say that in 'is day 'ee could 'ear it clear through to the Densim Pass.'

'That must have been Grandpa,' said Piper proudly. 'He could shatter conkers with his Voice, and he once burst the eardrums of a Vishis Fween with his famous high note.'

'That was yer Grandpa, was it indeed?' said Froshus in respectful awe, and then he suddenly remembered something. 'Did I 'ear you say you couldn't sing? I never 'eard of a Froom who couldn't sing. And what's gonna 'appen to the Song if you can't sing it?' he said in great consternation.

'Piper's going to find his Voice,' Snoot piped up. 'That's why we're going to Mount Florn. His Voice is being held prisoner by the Vishis Fween.'

'Mount Florn! The Vishis Fween! What am I 'earin? You little uns ain't no match for them monsters! Them Fweens is evil! An' they've bin gettin' peskier and peskier since the wolves left. The wolves is the only thing in the world they fear. Some of our clan's gone missin' recently. nippers too some of em, and I've 'erd of others that 'ave disappeared, snatched from their beds in the dead of night! And now I come to think of it, I ain't seen a Boodog for many a moon! Them Fweens is roofless, deevyus and malishus!'

'That's why we have to be there on the night of the full moon when the Voices will be unguarded,' said Piper. 'That's what Pierre told us.'

'Well, I 'ope 'ees right this Pierre!'

'Pierre does know everything,' Snoot added reassuringly.

'You mentioned the Boodogs Froshus,' said Piper. 'Grandpa talked about them once. He told me they live on the south slopes of Mount Florn.'

'And so they did but them Fweens 'as been pickin' em off, one by one!'

'Then it's a good job that the wolves are back!' exclaimed Piper.

At the look of surprise on Froshus' face there was nothing for it but to give a full account of their story. Piper told them everything and Froshus and the clan listened in fascination, punctuating the story throughout with 'oohs' and 'aahs' and 'good old Loupus!' and 'them Eagles is not to be trusted!' and 'a flying squirrel, oo'd a thought!'

'Well, I'm glad the wolves are back!' said Froshus when Piper had finished his story. 'P'raps they'll be able to do something about them varmints! Now, enough talk.

69

You poor little beggars look done in! If you're goin' to Mount Florn to rescue yer Voice, yer gonna need all yer strength. I'm guessin yer thinkin' of takin' the Densim Pass?' he added as an after thought.

'That's the plan,' said Piper. If we approach Mount Florn from the Plain we're too exposed to the Fweens. We'd never make it.'

Froshus was silent for a moment. He looked at them intently and then he seemed to make up his mind. 'If yer take the Densim Pass yer might not make it neither,' he said quietly. 'I know you 'ave ter go but you really is between the devil and the deep blue sea, as me old Ma used ter say.'

'What do you mean Froshus? What's out there on the Densim Pass?'

'I don't want to alarm yer cos there ain't too many of 'em, but . . . well . . . it's in'abited by the Fuming Wrath'oggs! They ain't evil like them Fweens but they're fiercer than a ragin' bull with an 'ead-ache! I wouldn't wanna tangle with 'em!'

Piper quailed at this unexpected piece of news. He and Snoot had been naive to imagine they could just trot off to Mount Florn, rescue his Voice and trot back home again. Snoot was looking at him in horror, but what was he to do?

'We have to take our chances on the Densim Pass,' he said at last. 'The other way just isn't an option.'

'Right! That's decided then!' said Froshus briskly. 'I wish it didn't 'ave ter be that way but it's clear that you 'ave to find yer Voice so let's 'ave no more about it for now. Jump to it boys, let's 'ave some food for the little uns. They're gonna need all their strength for tomorrer!'

The clan sprang into action and ran around making preparations for their unexpected guests. 'You'll be safe enough 'ere with us tonight,' said Froshus staring thoughtfully at the moon. 'You ain't got long though. Two nights tops I'd say!'

'Do you think we can make it?' Piper asked timidly.

'Of course yer can!' Froshus exclaimed. 'In all me days I never saw a braver Froom! Nor a braver Soozle neither!' he added, his eyes welling up with tears.

'Thank you Froshus,' said Piper swelling with pride. He knew that what they needed now above all else, was confidence and he knew that Froshus knew it too.

'Have you encountered many Soozles in these parts then Froshus?' asked Snoot expectantly.

'Well I 'ave to own up that yer the very first that I've ever clapped eyes on!' Froshus replied. Snoot's hopeful expression changed to one of disappointment.

'Your parents could be back home in the Lumbery Wood by now, wondering what's happened to you,' said Piper encouragingly.

'I never thought of that,' said Snoot brightening. 'You could be right!'

'Well now, you must be famished!' said Froshus springing into action and clapping his paws at the clan. 'Let's eat!'

While they ate, Froshus kept their spirits up by telling them tales of his clan's exploits, then Zoot-Alors, followed by the rest of the Ferrets, escorted them with great ceremony to his own burrow.

'Tonight I share weez Muggins,' he said proudly. 'You sleep very good in my 'ouse! Eez clean an' warm! Chomper here, he keep zee watch!'

'Thank you Zoot-Alors, it's very kind of you to give up your burrow. We'll certainly sleep well tonight,' said Piper. The whole clan stood by and watched while Piper and Snoot settled themselves into the burrow. Piper could hear them whispering to each other as they tiptoed off. 'SSSHHH! Them little uns is worn out!'

Piper tried to put the alarming thought of the Fuming Wrath'oggs out of his mind. There was no point in dwelling on it, they had to go on with the quest. Balance! Froshus had said. Piper had never thought of it like that but he was right! If there was no more Spring Wake-up Song then the creatures wouldn't wake up and the whole of the Wide River Valley would be out of balance.

Snoot had already dropped off to sleep, exhausted by the days events but Piper was restless and wakeful. There had been no trace of Snoot's parents along the way, nor of any other Soozle for that matter. Piper knew that Cracker and Stasha could take care of themselves and that they would never venture into the dangerous terrain of the Flornean Plain. He knew that Snoot knew it too, which is why he was sleeping like a baby while Piper lay awake worrying. He wondered what Grizel would be doing now. He hoped that she wouldn't take it upon herself to go after Betula! Mrs Eagle would have her for breakfast! This thought made his heart beat faster and he tossed and turned in Zoot-Alors' comfortable burrow, trying to rid his mind of terrifying thoughts. Eventually, a combination of sheer exhaustion and the reassuring snoring of Chomper, who was curled up outside the entrance, lulled him off to a deep and dreamful sleep.

When they emerged the next morning, Snoot refreshed and energetic, Piper bleary eyed and dozy, the clan was waiting to greet them. 'Bonjour mes amis,' said Zoot-Alors. I 'ope you 'ave good sleep?'

'Oh yes thank you,' Piper lied. 'Your burrow is very cozy.'

'There's no time to lose!' said Froshus dragging a beaming Zoot-Alors back into line with the rest of the clan. 'There's still a long way to go before yer reach the edge of the Forest of Mustela and then . . . well then there's the Densim Pass to neegoshate. Chomper'n Muggins'll go with yer to the borders. After that . . . well I wish yer luck an' I 'ope yer find what yer lookin' for,' he said, addressing himself to Snoot. Then he turned to Piper and said softly, 'if you 'ave courage you'll find yer Voice. Ere! Take this,' he said handing him a short bamboo phial plugged with a Quercus leaf. 'It might 'elp yer.'

'What is it?' asked Piper.

'Sleepin' potion. Speciality of the missis. Runs the infirm'ry my Patience! Keeps us all in good shape with 'er tonics and potions. One dose of them could drop an eflerant in less than 'alf a minute. She's been workin' on 'em since them Fweens became troublesome. Tested 'em on Rotter she did. 'Ee went down like a ton o' bricks and didn't wake up for four days! 'Aven't worked out what to do with 'em yet but they might come in 'andy in a tricky sichwayshun.' Piper took the phial and gave it a shake. 'Nokshus Berries, 'andle with care!' warned Froshus.

'I don't know how to thank you,' Piper said gratefully as he tucked the phial into the groove behind his ear where Betula had once rested.

'To 'ear you sing the Spring Wake-up Song'll be thanks enough for me,' replied Froshus. 'Now yer'd best be on yer way.'

It was comforting to have something that reminded him of Betula and Piper felt proud and honoured to have been helped by so many good hearted creatures. *I'll have something to tell Gnawberry when I get back home; if I get back home,* he thought solemnly.

In the company of Chomper and Muggins, the two friends said a reluctant goodbye to Froshus and the rest of the Ferret clan and set off once more on their journey.

Eleven

To The Densim Pass

The small clearing where the ferrets kept their camp was surrounded by dense forest and Piper soon realized, not for the first time, that without their guides they would have become hopelessly lost. The ancient trees closed in around them and great, gnarled roots rose up out of the ground and writhed and twisted their way across the forest floor like petrified serpents. Chomper and Muggins were accustomed to the forest and happily bounced their way through the jungle of limbs but Piper and Snoot had to climb and crawl through the tangled web and by midday they were battered, bruised and exhausted. The dark forest was oppressive, stifling and devoid of life. Nothing stirred, not even a weevil and the two friends were soon overwhelmed by a depressing sense of gloom.

'Do you think we'll ever get out of here Snoot?' Piper asked wearily.

'Well, if we don't it won't be long before I go completely mad!' Snoot exclaimed.

'There's a clearin' not far off,' said Chomper. 'We'll stop'n rest a bit.'

As they approached the clearing a tantalizing glimmer of light flickered through the branches and then at last, they were out of the trees and into a welcoming pool of brilliant sunshine. Piper raised his head to the sky and sighed with relief. 'I was beginning to think I'd never see the sun again,' he said.

'A perfect day for snail foraging,' Snoot said wistfully.

After a short rest and a bite to eat the reluctant travellers resumed their journey into the murky, sunless depths and it wasn't long before the uplifting effects of the sunshine wore off and the gloom closed in on them again. The way became even more laborious as they were now beginning the ascent of the mountain. Even the ferrets began to lose some of their earlier enthusiasm for the expedition as they approached the outer reaches of their territories. 'Our grandparents used to live 'ere but now all our kind 'ave their camps on the northern borders. There's no call f'rus to come 'ere anymore,' said Muggins.

'It doesn't look as if anyone comes here anymore,' said Piper gloomily. 'It's a wilderness!'

The further into the forest they ventured, the darker and more oppressive it became. It cast a spell of melancholy on them all. Even the cheerful ferrets had stopped their chattering and it seemed that no one had the will to speak. The grim lifeless place spread its aura of wretchedness through the company and they continued their tortuous journey in morose silence, each preoccupied with his own thoughts.

Doubt and uncertainty began to pervaded Pipers mind. *What if my Voice isn't there on Mount Florn! Everyone's depending on me now!* Piper sighed heavily as the weight of responsibility dragged at his weary body. *Why haven't my parents sent Pierre to look for me? They must have meant for me to go and find my Voice!* Piper began to panic. *How can I ever go home if I fail in my quest? 'It was HIS fault,' they'd all say. 'HE was the one responsible!* He could hear Snorky Trotter's voice saying, what a loser! Piper Froom, the only Froom in history that can't sing!' He wallowed in self pity for a while before his rambling thoughts turned to Loupus. He'd been barely more than a pup when his parents and his pack had deserted him; left him out there alone, to fend for himself. He began to feel ashamed. At least he wasn't alone.

As Piper battled with his dark thoughts, he was suddenly brought back to reality by a strong, pervading aroma. He'd grown accustomed to the pungent scent that accompanied his ferret companions but now a new odour assailed his nostrils. Snoot had picked it up too.

'What's that horrible smell?' he said sniffing the air. Piper knew what it was. He'd smelt it before. It was a scent known also to Chomper and Muggins who were now becoming increasingly alarmed.

'FWEENS!' they squealed in unison, searching frantically around them. The undergrowth had been flattened and trampled in a wide swathe which cut directly across their path.

'It looks like an 'ole tribe of 'em's tramped through 'ere,' said Chomper in horror. 'I've never seen the likes of this before! There must be 'undreds of 'em!'

'There are hundreds of them!' said Piper fearfully. 'I saw them from the Eagles nest.' Snoot's ears pricked up and he looked at Piper in surprise.

'Why didn't you tell me?' he demanded.

'I didn't want to worry you,' said Piper sheepishly, feeling guilty at the hurt look on Snoot's face.

'I don't like this one little bit!' said Chomper. 'There are other scents 'ere too and some of 'em's familiar. I'm getting a scent of ferret, an' blood 'n' fear all mixed up with Fween!' he exclaimed in alarm. 'I think it's Oderus's missis and their nipper! They went missin' a few nights ago.   Oderus thought she'd run off with one of them sneaky polecats and taken the nipper with her, but I don't like the look of this, no I don't!' he said shaking his head in disbelief.

Muggins who was doing some investigative sniffing a little way off, called to Chomper who bounced over to see what he'd found. Snoot remained aloof and Piper knew he had hurt his friend's feelings by not confiding in him. Neither of them spoke as they waited for the ferrets to finish their explorations. It wasn't long before Chomper and Muggins came bounding back.

'It looks like them Fweens passed by 'ere quite recent. We think they're headed off to the Old Wolves Trail which leads up to the caves, and they're takin' prisoners with 'em! You was right not to take that route but you'll be in grave danger when yer get to Mount Florn with them Fweens swarmin' all over! I don't like it one little bit, I don't,' said Muggins. 'If only yer could sing yer wouldn't 'ave to go through with yer quest. Couldn't yer just try?' he appealed to Piper.

'SING! NO, NO, I CAN'T SING!' squealed Piper in a panic. 'That's why I'm here remember!'

'I'm afraid it's true,' said Snoot in an aggrieved tone. 'I've heard him and he's really quite useless.'

Chomper and Muggins sighed and shook their heads sadly. They all stood around not knowing what to do next, reluctant to go on, reluctant to go back. It was Piper who finally made the decision.

'I'm going on with the quest,' he said quietly but firmly. 'I don't have any choice. There's no other Froom to take my place and Pa's too old and tired to carry on. I have to take my chances, but you don't have to risk your life for me Snoot. Go back with Chomper and Muggins. If I don't come back . . . well, you'll know what to do.' Snoot glared at Piper in disbelief.

'What kind of a friend do you take me for? Do you think I've come all this way for the good of my health? Did you really imagine that I'd skip off home and leave you here by yourself to face . . . Fweens and . . . and . . . Fuming Wrath'oggs and goodness knows what else! If that's what you think then you don't know me as well as you think you do! I wouldn't dream of leaving you by yourself, even if you do keep secrets from me. I'm shocked that you could even entertain such an idea! Besides,' he added grudgingly, 'without my navigating skills you'd be lost in no time.' Snoot puffed out his chest and stood his ground but the expression on his face gave away his injured feelings.

Piper sighed with relief. 'I never for one minute thought any of those things and I knew that you wouldn't leave me but . . . well . . . it had to be said . . . that's all.'

'Well then!' said Snoot who had a very forgiving nature. 'Onwards and upwards! Tomorrow night the moon will be full. We have until midnight until it reaches its zenith.'

'Aren't you afraid?' asked Piper.

'Of course I'm afraid,' Snoot replied, 'but we can be afraid together.' The ferrets had been watching this discourse taking place and now they both sniffed and Chomper wiped away a tear. 'No use arguin' then,' he said. 'But I'm afraid this is as far as we go. This is the very limit of our patch, we don't dare go no further.'

'Yer on yer own now,' said Muggins. 'Beyond them trees, lies the Densim Pass. Keep 'eadin' due South and don't stray from the path; the Pass 'arbours many a trech'rous ravine. Above all, don't make no noise! Them Fumin' Wrath'oggs 'ates noise! It stirs their 'orrible tempers and there's no tellin' what could 'appen!'

All the time Muggins had been talking, Chomper had been sniffing nervously around. Now he was impatient to be off. 'Are yer sure yer won't change yer mind and come back with us?' he begged.

'Sorry Chomper, but a Froom's got to do what a Froom's got to do,' said Piper in an attempt to lighten the mood. 'Besides, I've always got these if I get into a sticky sichwayshun,' he said taking the phial of Nokshus berries from behind his ear and giving it a shake.

'An' I 'ope yer never 'ave cause ter use 'em!' said Chomper. 'I suppose yer'd best be on yer way then,' he added reluctantly.

The ferrets finally dragged themselves away from their new friends and set off back to camp, waving and calling until they were out of sight. 'This is it then Snoot. It's just you and me again.'

'And those Nokshus berries which will come in very handy if we encounter an eflerant on our journey,' bantered Snoot.

'I'll bet there are hordes of them lying in wait for us,' Piper laughed. The prospect of coming face to face with a Fuming Wrath'ogg was not one that either of them dared to contemplate and their humour masked their fears. They were going to need all their fortitude if they were to make it through the Densim Pass and on to Mount Florn.

'Are you ready Snoot?' asked Piper, leading the way.

'It's now or never,' replied Snoot.

'Then the Densim Pass, here we come!'

Twelve

The Fuming Wrath'ogg

The ancient oaks now gave way to the dark trunks of tall firs which towered high above their heads. The dense canopy obscured the daylight and they clambered the steep slopes in semi darkness. They dared not speak for fear of alerting their presence to the Fuming Wrath'oggs. Piper stopped often to listen, his ears pricked for the slightest sound but all remained quiet. The day wore on without event and Piper was just beginning to hope that they would make it without mishap when he felt a strange sensation creeping up from his toes and through his body. He stopped in his tracks and pricked up his ears. Then his body began to shiver and shake and a low rumble like the sound of distant thunder rolled its way towards them like a gathering storm.

'Is it an earthquake?' cried Snoot in alarm. The rumble grew to a mighty roar and the ground began to shake violently. Then Piper screamed in terror, 'RUN SNOOT! RUN FOR YOUR LIFE!' as a huge and powerful Fuming Wrath'ogg came steaming through the forest towards them.

Piper ran so fast he thought his heart would burst. A cloud of choking dust enveloped him and he fled blindly and erratically through the dark forest, the snorting beast hard on his heels. It was so close to him now that he could feel the gust of it's hot breath on his back as it roared with anger. Then just when he thought he was going to die, he was flying through space his limbs flailing, clutching and grabbing at the air until his grasp found something solid and he held on for dear life.

He hung there swaying for some time before he plucked up the courage to look around. When he realized where he was it was almost as terrifying as the pursuit of the Fuming Wrath'ogg. The old tree that he'd managed to grab onto on his fall through space, grew out of a crevice in the sheer rock face and Piper found himself suspended over a yawning abyss. His head span sickeningly at the sight. This was worse than the Eagles nest and Grizel wouldn't be there to break his fall when he lost his grip. And where on earth was Snoot? Had he gone over the edge too? Piper didn't dare to think of it. First, he had to find a way out of this predicament. He looked up to see the Fuming Wrath'ogg staring wildly down at him, snorting and pawing angrily at the ground. It tossed it's huge head from side to side and long, slimy strands of slaver flobbed from its terrible tusks and plopped down into Piper's eyes, momentarily blinding him. He shook his head, trying to rid himself of the disgusting phlegm which ran down his face, then he steeled himself and looked down. His stomach churned at the sight of the seemingly bottomless chasm and it took all his strength of will not to be sick. The sweat which had broken out on his paws threatened to loosen his grip. He had to steady his nerve or he would slide into oblivion. He composed himself, took a deep breath and looked around. Below him a narrow ledge protruded from the sheer rock face. If he could work his way along the branch perhaps he could drop onto the ledge. It was a long way down but it was his only hope. Piper began to inch his way gingerly along the branch, keeping his eyes fixed on the rock in front of him. If he looked down he would be lost, if he looked up he risked being blinded again by the slobber of the Fuming Wrath'ogg who was still pawing the ground above.

He was a little over halfway when there was a loud crack and the branch began to sag under his weight. *Not now! Don't break now! I'm nearly there!* With a last mighty effort he reached the end of the branch and the rock face was almost within reach. *Just a little bit further!* But Piper's weight had been too much for the brittle old tree and its dry roots began to crack and snap. One by one they loosed their hold and soon Piper was hanging by the last fibrous thread. He had to make the drop before it gave way and took him with it into the abyss. It was further away than he'd thought but he steadied himself and prepared for the drop. *It's now or never,* he thought as he let go. He fell heavily, stumbled then teetered precariously on the edge before lunging forward onto his belly. He lay there too afraid to move, his heart pounding in his chest, relief flooding over him as he felt the hard, solid rock beneath him. As his fear subsided and he regained possession of wits, he sat up and looked around. Way up above him rose the sheer face of Mount Florn; below - nothing. The ledge was barely large enough to accommodate him. His relief turned to dismay when he realized that there was no way out.

The Fuming Wrath'ogg had apparently given up the chase and gone home as he could no longer hear its angry snorting. It didn't make any difference anyway, it couldn't get at him down there.

He now had time to think about Snoot. A lot of time, he reflected. Then a thought occurred to him and he checked behind his ear for the phial of Nokshus berries. Miraculously, it was still there. *Oh poor Snoot! He should have turned back when he had the chance. This is truly the end of the road. Ma and Pa will never know what happened to me. The quest is over and I've broken the balance!* Piper began to cry, silently and painfully until every fibre of his being ached. Then, as his sobs subsided he unplugged the phial of Nokshus Berries and poured them into his paw. There were three of them. Two, he put carefully back into the phial, just in case, and the third he held tightly in his paw. If he could just go to sleep and block out the pain. Four days Froshus had said. In four days anything could happen on that ledge. He had just about made up his mind when a voice came out of nowhere.

'Are you going to sit there blubbing all day?' Piper almost fell into the abyss in shock and surprise.

'Snoot!' he cried. 'Is that really you? But where on earth are you?'

'Up here!' Piper looked up and saw Snoot's head poking out from a fissure in the rock face just above him.

'Oh Snoot, I thought you'd gone over the edge! I thought I'd never see you again! But how did you get in there?'

'Climb up and I'll tell you,' said Snoot. Piper carefully replaced the Nokshus berry and put the phial back into the groove behind his ear. He looked up with dread at the sheer rock face and his legs turned to jelly.

'You can do it Piper, it's not that far,' said Snoot encouragingly.

Piper took a deep breath and steeled himself for the climb. Although it was only a short distance, one small slip and he would fall to his death in the abyss. By the time he reached the crack in the rock face he was trembling from head to foot. Snoot leaned out as far as he dared and hauled his friend to safety.

'Phew,' puffed Piper as he spread-eagled himself on the hard, comforting floor. 'I'm made for burrowing, not climbing!'

'You're safe now Piper, look!'

Piper sat up and looked around. 'It's a tunnel!' he said in surprise. But how on earth did you end up here?'

'While that Fuming Wrath'ogg was on your tail I dived for cover in a crevice,' Snoot explained. 'I heard you scream Piper! I thought you were dead!' He stopped, momentarily choked with emotion. 'I was too afraid to move. I could hear that beast pawing the ground and snorting and I thought it had killed you and was looking for me! I was so scared that I squeezed myself further and further into the crevice. That's when I realized that it opened up into this tunnel. I could see a pinpoint of daylight in the distance so I went to investigate. I thought it might offer an escape route from the Fuming Wrath'ogg. Imagine my surprise when I looked out of that hole and saw you Piper!'

'And I nearly jumped out of my skin when I heard your voice! I'd all but given up. But what do we do now? We can't go back to the Densim Pass, not with that beast lying in wait for us.'

'If there's one tunnel, it's possible there are others,' said Snoot. 'I headed straight here towards the light so I haven't had time to explore properly yet. You go first Piper, your underground senses are better than mine.'

Piper beamed with pride as he squeezed past his friend to take the lead. He stood for a moment sniffing the air and feeling the walls around him. Although narrow, the tunnel appeared to be high and the air flowed freely. 'Stay close Snoot, I don't want to risk losing you again.'

'Ready when you are!' said Snoot. 'Onwards and Upwards.'

As they advanced into the tunnel leaving the daylight behind, Piper used his well developed senses to find his way through the darkness. There were indeed many fissures in the craggy walls but so far all had proved to be dead ends. They were almost back to the point at which Snoot had entered through the crevice when Piper stopped, put his snout in the air and sniffed.

'Do you feel that Snoot? There's a current of air coming from somewhere. I think I might have found a tunnel.' He ran his paws over the cold moist rock until he felt something; or rather he felt nothing.

'It's here Snoot! A hole large enough to crawl through and I can feel the air from the other side!'

'Lead on Piper, I'm right behind you.'

Piper got down on his belly and wriggled his way through the crack. There was barely room to move but he dragged himself steadily forwards. He hoped to see a glimmer of daylight which might indicate a way out but it remained as black as pitch. Then suddenly, without any warning, there was nothing beneath him and once again he found himself tumbling through space. He almost had time to reflect that this was becoming a habit when he landed with a sickening thud which knocked all the wind out of him. Before he could catch his breath, something landed heavily on top of him.

'Piper! Piper! Where are you?' came an indistinct cry. Piper mustered what little puff he had left and hauled himself out from under his friend.

'Oh there you are! Are you all right? Are you hurt?'

'I think I'll live,' panted Piper trying to catch his breath. 'What about you? Are you ok?'

'I had a soft landing, thank you,' said Snoot sheepishly. 'I wonder where we are now?' he mused.

'I don't know, but I do know that it isn't where I was hoping to be. It seems that we're even deeper inside the mountain; but if that's the case then why can I see you?'

'I can see you too,' said Snoot in surprise.

Piper got to his feet and looked around. As his eyes became accustomed to the soft glow, a strange and fantastic sight began to emerge. What he saw made him gasp in wonder.

Thirteen

The Plight of the Boodogs

'Just look at that Snoot. Have you ever seen anything so . . . so . . . breathtaking?'

The tunnel had led them into in a cavern of gigantic proportions. Magnificent, glistening pinnacles hung from the roof like giant icicles. The same incredible forms grew up from the floor and where the two met, colossal columns rose up in majestic splendour, forming beautiful grottos and chambers. The soft glow which dimly illuminated the cavern came from the strange mushroom like growths which draped the glistening walls with their frilly capes. An underground lake rippled with the continuous musical drip, drop of the melting pinnacles.

'It's magical,' whispered Snoot in wonder.

As they gazed mesmerized by the wondrous sight, a long, shrill whistle pierced the air and the dark roof above their heads suddenly began to roll and swirl. Then it surged towards them and Piper and Snoot were engulfed by a black tidal wave of shrieking bats and the din of thousands of beating wings echoed deafeningly around the walls. Then as quickly as they had roused, the bats were gone. It took the friends a few moments to recover from their shock and in the quiet that followed, they became aware that they were not alone.

'There's something out there,' hissed Piper in a trembling voice.

'What is it?' whispered Snoot clinging to Piper.

down here. This is all that remains of our colony,' said Mot looking sadly around at the small gathering of thin and sorry Boodogs. 'Many have died since coming down here and very soon there will be none of us left; unless a miracle happens,' he said looking searchingly at Piper.

'But how did you come to be here?' asked Snoot.

'Well my friend, that's a long story,' said Mot sinking wearily to the ground beside the old Boodog. 'This is Grog and I'm going to need his help to tell our story.'

He waited until everyone was settled and comfortable (for this was the whole of the Boodog history), and then he began to tell their story.

'Boodogs have lived contentedly on the south slopes of Mount Florn for as far back as anyone can remember. Our losses were due mainly to illness or old age, or perhaps now and again an over adventurous youngster might wander too far from home and the eagles would seize their opportunity, but our colony was large, and strong and healthy. The wolves kept mainly to the Plain and were rarely bothersome; they hunted only to survive.

Then the Fweens came. They were drawn to Mount Florn because of the strength of our numbers. They took over the caves on the north side of the mountain and whenever they were hungry or bored, they came looking for us. There weren't so many of them back then and the wolves kept their numbers under control, but there were enough of them to ruin our lives. They're vicious, unnatural beasts who kill indiscriminately for pleasure. It goes against the laws of nature! They took many of our innocent babies, and their mothers were so traumatized by the loss of their little ones that they became easy prey for the cowardly and unscrupulous Fweens. I was just a youngster myself and my mother lived in fear of losing me to the beasts. We were forced to hide away until we were prisoners in our own burrows; but we had to eat, so we developed a system of surveillance. We fed only in the afternoons when the Fweens were at their laziest, and the strongest amongst us would act as lookouts. We Boodogs are good whistlers and the lookouts soon worked out an alarm system to warn of approaching danger. The system worked and we were able to feed but we'd lost our freedom and we lived in constant fear. We'd resigned ourselves to this miserable existence and then one day a miracle happened. He came along!'

Mot fell silent. His part in the story was apparently at an end. Piper and Snoot had been listening with rapt attention, horrified by the despicable deeds of the Fweens and the suffering of the poor Boodogs.

'But what was the miracle and who was he?' Piper wanted to know. The Boodogs, who knew that Grog was always deeply moved by their story, remained silent and waited patiently while he gathered his thoughts and took up the story.

'I was on lookout duty that day,' he began, addressing Piper. 'I remember it as if it were yesterday. There he came, as bold as a Jackdaw, not a care in the world! I couldn't believe my eyes. The Fweens had just woken from their usual afternoon nap and were preparing for a foray. He couldn't see them as the path veered sharply round the mountain and the wind must have been in the wrong direction. If you've ever been close to a Fween you'd know what I'm talking about,' he said wrinkling his nose in disgust.

'But who was he?' Piper insisted, his curiosity getting the better of his patience.

'I'm just coming to that,' said Grog, 'all in good time.' Piper waited as patiently as he could while Grog got up and stretched his cramped legs, then making himself comfortable again, he picked up where he'd left off.

'Then quite suddenly,' he continued, 'he must have caught a whiff of them because he put his snout in the air and sniffed and I could see his whole body stiffen with fear. The Fweens were getting closer and they'd got wind of him. The new and unfamiliar scent worked them up and they would have torn him to shreds in seconds if I hadn't acted quickly. I did the only thing I knew. As the Fweens rounded the corner I whistled, as sharp and as high as I could muster. They don't like shrill sounds, it hurts their ears, but it distracted them long enough for him to recover his wits. I've never in my life seen anything as brave and as quick witted as that small creature faced with those evil, vicious Fweens. He saw their discomfort at my whistle and he used it to his advantage. He lifted his head, opened his mouth and let out a note so pure and high that it could have pierced a hole through to the middle of Mount Florn! My ears still ring with it to this day.'

'Grandpa!' whispered Piper in astonishment. So the story was true!

'The Fweens went berserk,' went on Grog Boodog. 'Their leader, the Vishis Fween, who'd been nearest the Froom . . . yes the Froom, for that's what he was,' he said nodding to Piper, 'fell to the ground writhing in agony, his legs kicking out in all directions and foaming at the mouth like a rabid dog. The others turned tail and fled, screaming in pain. The Vicious Fween lay there comatose; no one dared go near him. The next day he was gone. We suspect that the wolves took him as there were signs of a body being dragged away.

That Froom gave us back our lives! We begged him to stay but he said he was on an adventure and that he still had things to explore.

For a while life was good again. Our freedom was restored and we could come and go as we pleased but our colony was depleted. Then the wolves left! Somehow, the Fweens must have got to know about it because not long after, they returned this time in their droves. We were forced underground again. We knew that we couldn't withstand another onslaught so we came here to save what was left of our numbers. We've always known about these caverns and tunnels. Mount Florn is riddled with them. That was many moons ago and we'd given up all hope of having our lives back; until today! Today, you came along and now we can hope again,' said Grog Boodog earnestly.

Mot and the others looked yearningly at Piper. Their very existence depending upon him, a small and timid Froom who couldn't sing.

Piper was overwhelmed. *I know what they're asking of me but I can't help them*, he thought desperately. *Grandpa was a hero, fearless and brave. How could I ever live up to him?* It didn't occur to Piper that he had his Grandfather's blood running through his veins, or that he was unwittingly following in his footsteps. He instinctively felt for Betula's comforting presence but his paw closed instead around the bamboo phial which still nestled behind his ear. *Who am I kidding*, he thought. *Even if I still had Betula, she couldn't save a colony of Boodogs! Oh what am I going to do?* They were all looking at him expectantly. He had to tell them something but he didn't want to be the one to dash their hopes forever.

It was Snoot who finally broke the silence. 'We came here to find Piper's singing Voice,' he said boldly. 'We believe that it is here on Mount Florn being held prisoner by the Vishis Fween.' An alarmed muttering went round the darkening cave.

'Find his singing voice, what does he mean? Can it be possible that we've pinned all our hopes on the only Froom alive who can't sing? Oh no, no, we're surely doomed!' the Boodogs wailed.

The rosy evening glow that had permeated the chamber had long since faded to night and Piper could just make out through the gloom, the humped, dejected forms of the defeated Boodogs. Mot and Grog Boodog stared at the floor in an attitude of utter despair. Piper could feel their wretchedness as they realized that the glimmer of hope that he'd brought to their lives, had been extinguished forever. He was overwhelmed by a nauseating sense of uselessness and failure as the silence was broken only by the choking sobs of the condemned creatures. Now he needed his Voice more than ever! Not only for the Spring Wake-up Song and for Pa and to keep the balance, but also to defeat the Fweens.

Piper's whole body sagged and his head slumped listlessly onto his chest. He realized with dismay that he'd lost his determination for the quest, out there on the ledge when he'd thought that Snoot was dead and that he himself was going to die. The burden of responsibility was too much to bear. He was just one small, insignificant Froom who couldn't sing. What could he do against the Fweens.

In the moments that followed, the atmosphere in the chamber was heavy with despair; but Snoot wasn't giving up that easily. 'We came here to find Piper's Voice and that is exactly what we're going to do! Tomorrow night, when the moon is full, my friend here will have his Voice!' Piper stared at him aghast. What did Snoot think he was doing? Here they were, trapped deep in the heart of the mountain. What chance did they have of finding their way out before tomorrow night!

Just at that moment the moon appeared, full and bright in the opening high up in the chamber wall. Framed in the round hole, it beamed down on them like a gigantic eye. For a minute or two it fixed its gaze on Piper, challenging him, testing his mettle. Piper looked around at the expectant faces, illuminated by the moon's beam. Snoot had rekindled their dreams. He turned to his friend who was looking at him with a fierce pride and determination and he felt something stirring deep down inside himself; something strange and unexplainable. Then he remembered Loupus' words; *what good is a life without hope? I may not be brave like Grandpa,* he thought, *and I may not have a Voice like Pa's but at least I can give them hope. Anything has to be better than this miserable resignation.*

'Snoot's right,' he said with as much conviction as he could muster. 'That's my quest, to find my Voice and that's what I intend to do. If we can find a way out of here I'll do everything in my power to help you!' Piper sensed the Boodogs spirits rise. He sensed their hopes emerging from the ruins of their lives. He had to start believing again in his quest.

Suddenly, Mot jumped to his feet. 'Wait a minute!' he said excitedly. 'Did you say the Voices were here, on Mount Florn?'

'Yes, that's what Pierre told Piper. That the Voices were being held prisoner and on the night of the full moon, they would be left unguarded. That's why we have to get there tomorrow night!'

'Then I think we can help,' said Mot animatedly. 'I think we've heard them. We didn't realize what we were hearing but that must be it.'

'Yes, yes! That must be it! We've heard them, we've heard them,' the Boodogs chimed excitedly. The mood in the chamber had suddenly changed from one of doom and gloom to one of optimism and hope. Piper and Snoot were not immune to the atmosphere. They too needed to feel hope if they were to succeed in the quest.

'One of the tunnels on the north side, backs onto the cave of the Vishis Fween,' Mot explained. 'We know it's his cave because there's a crack in the wall and we can smell his vile odour. It's through this crack that we've heard strange calls and cries which definitely don't come from the Fweens. These caverns, caves and tunnels run all the way through Mount Florn. Small creatures like us can get in through the crevices but as far as we know, there is only one way out and that's through the Cavern of the Thundering Falls. It lies on the other side of the mountain, a good day's trek from here. It's invisible to the outside world, hidden as it is behind the Falls. When we were stronger we used to venture out that way in search of food but it soon became too dangerous. We were too close to the Fweens and we couldn't risk them picking up our scent.'

'But don't the Fweens know about the Cavern?' asked Piper anxiously.

'Luckily for us they hate water and never venture near the Falls so we reckon that it's safe enough,' Mot replied.

'Behind the Falls a narrow ledge runs around the inside of the canyon. It's treacherous! One false step and it's a fall to certain death on the rocks below. Once beyond the Falls the track opens out and winds sharply around the north face of the mountain. From there it's just a short distance to the cave of the Vishis Fween where the Voices are imprisoned. Further down the track are the smaller caves where the rest of the tribe lives. Tomorrow we will take to you to the Tunnel of the Voices, but now we must rest. We will need all our strength for the journey and for whatever else we may encounter before the day is out.'

There was an undercurrent of suppressed excitement as the creatures settled themselves down for the night, each with his own hopes, dreams, doubts and fears. Tomorrow would tell! Tomorrow it would be all or nothing!

Unable to sleep, Piper lay on the floor of the cave, and looked up at the starry sky. The moon had slipped away and he imagined it observing the world from the heavens. Would the moon be looking down on his worried parents? Would it see Loupus reunited with his pack? He imagined it beaming down on the clearing as it had done on the night they'd found themselves in the ferret camp. Would Grizel look at the moon and think of him?

Snoot lay curled up on the floor beside Piper. Sleep eluded him too. The Boodogs were restless but slept from sheer exhaustion and their gentle snoring lent an air of normality to the night. From far away, somewhere out on the Flornean Plain, came the plaintive but reassuring howling of a wolf.

Then a more sinister sound began to reach the ears of the two wakeful friends. As it came nearer the night was suddenly filled with the terrifying sound of the half-crazed Fweens as they whooped and screamed their way up the mountain track. The Boodogs stirred but didn't wake. They had grown accustomed to the noise of the roistering tribe.

'I'm scared Snoot,' whispered Piper.

'Me too,' Snoot whispered back.

'Do you think . . . that Pierre's story was true? That the Fweens will leave the mountain tomorrow night?'

'If the Boodogs have heard the Voices, then his story must be true,' Snoot whispered.

Piper closed his eyes, buried his head in his paws and tried to shut out the sounds and the thoughts that threatened to overwhelm him. Tomorrow night when the moon was full, it would all be over. One way or another!

Fourteen

In the Tunnel of the Voices

As Piper awoke a pale light suffused the chamber and silhouetted the figures of the Boodogs as they stood over him.

'We thought we'd let you sleep,' said Mot.

'They've been up since first light waiting for you to wake up,' said Snoot. 'They're ready for off!'

'We're ready for off! Yes, yes! Ready for off!' they chattered excitedly. The poor dispirited creatures of yesterday seemed to have found a new energy. Piper felt guilty when he looked at their hopeful, trusting faces. It seemed that the whole world was depending upon him. He didn't know what today would bring and he felt weary with the weight of responsibility but he couldn't let it show. He couldn't dash their hopes. 'Well, then I'm ready for off too!' he said springing energetically to his feet. 'Lead the way Mot. The Voices are waiting!'

Mot Boodog knew his way around the bewildering labyrinth of tunnels, caverns and chambers. 'When I was stronger I explored these caves from end to end in search of a solution to our hopeless situation,' he explained as they set off on their trek through the mountain. 'In the end, all I could do was hope for a miracle.'

'Miracles can happen,' said Snoot looking from Mot to Piper.

'It's a miracle that you're here!' said Mot. 'But you never told us how you came to be here.'

As they journeyed through the subterranean maze, Piper and Snoot passed the time by telling their story to the attentive Boodogs who wanted to know every little detail of their adventures.

'And here's us only thinking about ourselves!' said Mot when Piper had finished. 'You're quite right about the Spring Wake-up Song! There's more at stake than just our lives. But the Densim Pass . . . and escaping a Fuming Wrath'ogg! That's quite a feat! Quite a feat!' Mot whistled in admiration. 'It seems that you've had an eventful journey, and it's not over yet,' he said thoughtfully.

'There can't be anything worse than a Fuming Wrath'ogg, can there?' said Snoot.

'Only the Fweens, but they won't be there,' said Piper, hoping with all his heart that his words would prove to be true.

The expedition through the bowels of Mount Florn was laborious and exhausting. They'd crawled through cracks and narrow tunnels of hard jagged rock, they'd scaled walls, slid down shafts and even waded up to their necks in icy cold water, the smallest amongst them having to be carried on the shoulders of the strongest. Some of the tunnels had opened out into spectacular grottos of breathtaking beauty but they'd been too preoccupied to notice. They were all exhausted and weak from hunger, having had nothing to eat all day but mushrooms. It seemed that these caves would never end. By the time they arrived at the Tunnel of the Voices, the Boodogs were done in.

Having reached their goal they slumped exhausted to the ground and Piper and Snoot waited while Mot struggled to catch his breath. They too were tired and hungry but they'd longed all day for this moment. Piper's heart was thumping. He was so close to his Voice, yet still so far away.

'On the other side of this wall is the cave of the Vishis Fween,' Mot said at last. 'If you listen carefully you can hear the Voices.'

Piper pressed his ear to the crack in the wall. A vile stench wafted on the musty air but he couldn't hear anything. Snoot was crouching beside him, listening. It seemed an eternity that Piper waited for the sound he so longed to hear. He was just beginning to lose hope when suddenly, there it was! The muffled but unmistakable sound of Voices was coming from the other side of the tunnel wall.

'Did you hear that Snoot?' Piper gasped. 'But what's wrong with them? They sound so piteous and desperate and they're meant to be entrancing and mesmerizing.' Snoot stared open mouthed at Piper, shocked at what he'd just heard.

'If the Voices aren't mesmerizing, then the Fweens won't leave the mountain and if the Fweens don't leave the mountain . . . ?'

The Boodogs had been listening intently to this exchange and in their weakened state, defeat quickly overwhelmed them. 'I'm sorry but you're on your own from here on in,' said Mot breathlessly. 'We're too weak to go any further.' He looked helplessly at Piper, the pleading in his eyes speaking more than words. 'Go find your Voice,' he said tremblingly. 'It's almost over, don't give up now. When the moon reaches its zenith the Voices will become mesmerizing, you'll see. Just one more tunnel then you're into the Cavern of the Thundering Falls. Go!' he said with his last ounce of strength. Then his eyes closed and his head drooped wearily onto his chest as sleep overtook him.

'We have to move fast,' said Snoot as he started to make his way back through the tunnel. 'The moon must be up by now. We may already be too late!'

'But Snoot, didn't you hear the Voices,' said Piper catching him up. 'What can I do with a miserable, dejected Voice? I need an enchanting Voice; a mesmerizing Voice; a strong, high Voice like Pa's and Grandpa's! Oh what am I going to do?' he wailed in despair.

'What we're going to do is to get what we came for,' said Snoot. 'Your Voice is out there Piper, you just have to believe in it. I'd rather die than give up now! So many creatures are depending on us. On you! We'd never forgive ourselves if we didn't at least try.'

They pressed on in silence, Snoot hurrying on ahead while Piper scuttled along behind. *Maybe Snoot's right and I have to start believing in myself,* he thought. *After all, everyone else believes in me, why shouldn't I? Grizel would think me a quitter!* It was this sobering thought that reasserted his famous determination.

'Of course you're right,' he said eventually, catching up with his friend. 'I'd rather die too, though I'd prefer not to,' he added. We've come this far, let's go and get what we came for!'

'Onwards and upwards then?' said Snoot relieved that his friend had regained his resolve.

'It's now or never,' said Piper doggedly. 'I can hear the falls, we must be nearly there. Whatever happens Snoot at least we'll be able to breathe fresh air again.'

As they rounded the bend, the end of the tunnel should have been in sight but there was only the merest chink of light to indicate that it was even there.

'Oh no!' cried Snoot. It must be a rock fall! We're trapped Piper!'

As they approached the blockage, Piper reached for Snoot and pulled him back. 'That's no rock fall,' he hissed.

'Then what on earth is it?' Snoot whispered back.

'I think it's a Greavil,' said Piper, his voice heavy with misgiving. Grandpa told me about them. They're giants that roam the mountain ranges in search of seclusion. They can't get along with each other, or anyone else for that matter. Grandpa said that they're the grumpiest creatures on the face of the earth but he told me they'd all but died out.'

'I AIN'T DEAD AN' I AIN'T DEAF NEIVER!' roared the obstruction which had apparently been dozing. It was the biggest creature that either of them had ever clapped eyes on and it filled the tunnel almost to the roof.

'I COME 'ERE FOR A BIT O' PEACE AND QUIET AN' WHAT DO I FIND?. . . WELL? . . . WHAT DO I FIND?' he roared.

'Soozle, I'm a Soozle, said Snoot jumping in alarm, and this is . . .'

'SOOZLE! I 'ate Soozle! Too pretty, pretty! All that silky 'air an' teef an' stuff. YOU!' he roared, stabbing a long, hairy finger at Piper.

'Froom, I'm a Froom,' squealed Piper.

'FROOM! I 'ate's them the most! All that sweet, sickly singin! Too nice! I 'ate things what's NICE!'

'But I can't sing,' Piper ventured in the hope that this might soften the Greavil up a bit.

'YOU WHAT! YOU'RE 'AVIN' A LARF! In all me days I ain't never 'erd of a Froom what can't sing! Well, well well!' he roared with laughter.

'But I came here to find my Voice which is being held prisoner in the cave of the Vishis Fween and I have to get it tonight, when the moon is full because I . . . '

'OVER MY DEAD BODY!' thundered the Greavil, suddenly losing his sense of humour. 'I 'ATES CREATURES WHAT'S COME 'ERE DISTURBIN' ME! Them Fweens though! Them Fweens is ADMIRABLE! Vile, filthy, stinkin', sneaky, cowardly, vicious, ADMIRABLE!'

While the Greavil was going through his list of the Fweens' admirable traits, Snoot whispered urgently to Piper. 'What are we going to do? We're running out of time.'

Piper had been thinking. 'Nokshus berries!' he said. 'If I can just get him to eat one.'

'Rotten, evil, dastardly, wicked, obnoxious, ADMIRABLE!' the Greavil went on. While he was speaking Piper took the phial with a flourish, from behind his ear and began shaking it in a disinterested manner. 'WHAT'S THAT YOU GOT THERE?' bellowed the Greavil.

'What? . . . Oh this? . . . It's nothing,' said Piper. 'Just some NICE, sweet, juicy berries. You wouldn't like them.'

'TOO RIGHT I WOULDN'T! I 'ate's berries!' Piper's heart sank. *Now what am I going to do?* he thought. The Greavil seemed to have fallen into a silent sulk. Then he suddenly perked up.

'Juicy you say? . . . An' sweet? . . . I bet them's VILE an' you're keepin' 'em all to yourself! Give 'em 'ere,' he said snatching at the phial. Piper ducked as the huge fist whistled past his ear.

'You could try one, first. To see if you like them. If you do you can have them all,' said Piper.

'Prap's you're right! They might be Vile . . . but then again . . . they might be . . . Nice,' he shuddered. 'Gimme one,' he said thrusting out a filthy, hairy hand. Piper unplugged the phial and carefully tipped one Nokshus berry into the Greavil's grimy palm. The Greavil took it between his thumb and forefinger, held it up for inspection, sniffed it, then popped it into his mouth and swallowed. Piper and Snoot held their breaths.

'THAT AIN'T NICE, THAT'S VI. . . ' His eyes began to roll, then his head lolled forward, then his whole body slumped sideways to the ground. Piper and Snoot looked at each other in amazement as the Greavil began to snore loudly and vibrantly.

'Nokshus berries came in 'andy in a tricky sichwayshun,' said Snoot, imitating Froshus.

'And I've still got two left! Lets get out of here in case he wakes up,' said Piper urgently. As quickly as they could, they clambered their way over the mountainous form of the sleeping giant and entered the Cavern of the Thundering Falls.

Fifteen

The Spell of the Moonbow

Inside the cavern, Piper and Snoot were deafened by the roar from the mighty cascade. The opening was immense and beyond it fell a curtain of thundering water which plummeted with torrential force to the rocky ravine far below. The air was wet with the misty spray which drifted on the night breeze, drenching their fur and stinging their eyes. Behind the falls, just as Mot had described, was a narrow ledge which hugged the sheer sides of the canyon.

'This is it then! Stay close!' Piper yelled as he steeled himself to step out onto the ledge. He edged his way cautiously, his back pressed hard against the ice cold rock, not daring to look down into the seething foam below. The canyon walls ran with water, forming rivulets which spilled down across the ledge making it treacherous and slippery. Snoot followed closely behind. The magnificence and sheer force of the crashing water almost overwhelmed them but they had to keep going. If they lost their nerve now it would all be over.

It was a great relief when they emerged at last from the canyon and left the Thundering Falls behind. Here the path opened out and they were able to continue side by side, although the roar of the falls was still deafening. As they rounded the north face of Mount Florn, the noise from the torrent abated and they were at last able to speak.

'The moon's already up Snoot,' said Piper in surprise. Snoot looked up at the night sky.

'Look Piper, a moonbow!' Piper followed his gaze. There across the moonlit sky, a perfect, silver arc bridged the horizon, and spanned the Flornean Plain from end to end. Piper gasped in astonishment. He had never seen anything so beautiful. He was lost in the moment, suddenly oblivious to the dangers which lay ahead. The unearthly beauty and unexpectedness of that silver moonbow made his flesh tingle and his fur stand on end. A mixed sensation of suspense and purpose stirred deep inside him making him feel dazed and giddy.

Then the spell was broken abruptly by the dark silhouette of a great bird which swooped low over their heads. The huge wings beat the air with a rhythmic whoosh, whoosh, whoosh and its harsh scream split the night. Then it turned and made off in the direction of the Flornean Plain.

'That was Mr Eagle,' said Piper, rudely shaken out of his trance. 'But why would he be flying at night?'

'I don't know,' said Snoot, 'but I do know that we haven't much time. Mot said that it wasn't far from here to the cave of the Vishis Fween. Listen to that Piper! Can you hear them?'

'I can hear them all right! They sound . . . excited . . . and . . . crazy!' Piper shuddered with horror and revulsion at the sound of the roistering Fweens on the plateau below. Then from far away on the Flornean Plain a lone wolf howled. *Loupus!* thought Piper. *Oh, I wish he were here now!* Suddenly, a familiar and pungent odour wafted by his nostrils, reminding him of what he had to do.

'Come on Snoot! Let's go, before I change my mind,' he said determinedly.

Although the moon was bright, it rose up behind Mount Florn and the mountain cast its dark shadow over their path. Their noses told them they were nearing the cave of the Vishis Fween but when it loomed darkly in front of them, Piper and Snoot stopped dead in their tracks. They clung together, their fur standing on end and their legs turning to jelly at the sight of the yawning black hole. The fetid stench mingled rankly with the unmistakable odour of fear and from the depths of the cave came the same desolate cries that they'd heard from inside the tunnel. Piper tried to speak but fear trapped the words in his throat. Then came a sound more dreadful than the desolate Voices; more dreadful than the crazed Fweens on the plateau below. A deep throaty growl rumbled from inside the cave and exploded in a thundering roar as the burning red eyes and the slavering jaws of the Vishis Fween, thrust themselves through the darkness.

'WHO DARES SHOW HIS FACE AT MY CAVE!' he roared, his lips curled back in a ferocious snarl, slaver dripping from his deadly, yellow fangs. Piper and Snoot leaped back in terror and in doing so, tumbled over the rocky outcrop and fell on top of each other. Trapped and unable to move they watched in horror as the Vishis Fween emerged from the cave and slunk towards them, his huge head and powerful shoulders swaying from side to side as he sought out the trespassers.

'I SMELL FRESH MEAT!' he bellowed as he bore down on them.

There was no escape. Piper could feel its hot, foul breath on his face and a drool of saliva plopped from the slavering jaw onto his chest. He closed his eyes and waited for the end to come.

Sixteen

The Desolate Voices

At that moment the full moon emerged above the summit of Mount Florn and illuminated the scene below in all its horror. As Piper stared up into the gaping jaws of the Vishis Fween, a large yellow bird swooped, flapping and squawking round its head. 'Get away from them you ugly, vile brute!' it screeched. The startled Fween leaped at the bird snapping and snarling, its attention momentarily diverted from its terrified victims.

'Pierre!' Piper cried out as a shower of yellow feathers billowed all around. As he gazed up in amazement, a dark shadow passed silently over their heads and then from on high came the whoosh, whoosh of the Eagle's mighty wings. The Vishis Fween looked up in shock and surprise. The formidable talons found their mark and tore savagely at the Fweens upturned face. Pierre fluttered to the ground, breathless and shaken but otherwise unharmed.

'Grizel! Grizel! Drop it now!' he squawked, to the dark shadow as it passed overhead.

'Piper! Catch!' shouted Grizel as she threw him the stick. 'Take Betula and get out! Get out now while you still can!' she shrieked at them. Then she turned and flew off in the direction of the Flornean Plain.

'Grizel!' Piper yelled after her, but she was already out of sight. Betula had fallen just out of reach, her whiteness shining tantalizingly in the moonlight. Mr

Eagle, having succeeded in ripping off half of the beast's ear, was now circling overhead in readiness for another attack.

Piper stood transfixed with horror as the bewildered Fween writhed in agony, blood gushing from its lacerated ear. Roaring with pain and anger, the beast stumbled blindly to its knees and Piper saw his chance. He ran and snatched up Betula then hurled himself towards the Vishis Fween.

'No Piper! No!' screamed Snoot in terror as he watched his friend run headlong towards the crazed monster. As the Vishis Fween gave a mighty roar, Piper jammed Betula with all his might, into the gaping jaws of the astounded beast. Then, in one deft move, he plucked the phial from behind his ear, pulled out the leafy plug and poured the Nokshus berries down the fearsome throat. The Vishis Fween gurgled and choked, his eyes wide with disbelief, then he began to sway from side to side before finally crashing unconscious to the ground.

Piper and Snoot stared in astonishment at the bloodied, sprawled out body, its great yawning jaw held open by a small, white stick. 'Gnawberry was right, Betula did save our lives,' whispered Piper in a daze. 'And Grizel brought her to me, just like she said she would!'

'But it was you Piper! You, who saved us!' gasped Snoot in awe and admiration.

Pierre, having picked himself up and rearranged his disheveled feathers, was now flapping frantically around their heads. 'Go! Get out of here before it's too late,' he squawked. 'The wolves are coming!'

'But the Voices!' cried Piper.

'Too dangerous to stay here! Go! Go! Go!' shrilled Pierre in a panic, then he flew off in great haste to the Flornean Plain, calling as he went . . . 'Go . . . go . . . go . . .'

It had all happened so fast that Piper and Snoot were still reeling from the shock. 'The Voices! We have to release the Voices!' Piper said, coming back to his senses. 'Look at the moon Snoot, we don't have much time!'

Snoot gazed fearfully at the dark, forbidding mouth of the cave. 'What if there are more of those . . . those . . . monsters inside?'

'We have to take that chance, but judging from the din, I'd say that they're all down there on the plateau,' said Piper. 'I don't know what they're doing but I don't like the sound of it. I'm frightened Snoot, I don't mind telling you, but there's no going back now. I came here to find my Voice and I'm not going home without it!'

'I'm frightened too Piper and I really hope you're right about the Fweens being on the plateau, but I suppose there's only one way to find out. Are you ready Piper?' said Snoot taking a deep breath.

'As ready as I can be,' said Piper, preparing himself.

As they crept fearfully into the mouth of the cave the nauseating stench stung their nostrils and threatened to overwhelm them. Too afraid to venture any further, they cowered indecisively in the entrance. The rising moon suddenly beamed a pool of unworldly light on the cavern floor and cast their shadows in front of them. From the darkness beyond came the heart rending cries and desperate sobs of the imprisoned Voices. This was the moment that Piper had longed for but now that it was here he was afraid. 'This isn't how I dreamed it would be,' he whispered. 'They sound so desolate and pitiful!'

He took a deep breath and called out tremulously to the darkness beyond. 'Hello there.' The Voices fell silent. 'Hello!' He called out again. The Voices began to whisper; then there was a scurrying and a scuttering from the back of the cave. Piper held his breath. He didn't know what he was going to find and he was terrified at what might manifest itself from the darkness. Then suddenly a Voice spoke out.

'Piper? Piper Froom? Is that you?'

Piper and Snoot gasped in disbelief at the sound of that Voice. It was Snoot who cried out. 'Ma? Is that you? Is it really you?'

'Snoot! Oh my Snoot!' cried the Voice, and two dark shapes emerged from the darkness and threw themselves upon Snoot almost knocking him to the floor.

'Ma! Pa! Am I dreaming? I thought I'd never see you again!' cried Snoot and he broke down and sobbed as he was reunited with his lost parents.

Piper was staring open mouthed at this miraculous event and he didn't notice that a host of disheveled and desperate creatures had emerged from out of the shadows. What in the world were Cracker and Stasha Soozle doing here? A movement caught his attention and he looked up to see his desperate and desolate Voices standing expectantly before him. There was an array of small defenseless creatures, most of them mothers, desperately clutching their youngsters to them in terror of them being snatched away. Amongst them was a She Ferret with a baby, who Piper took to be Oderus' missis and nipper.'

'Help us! Please help us!' they pleaded. 'The Vishis Fween is going to kill us!'

'It's all right,' said Piper reassuringly, 'he won't be coming back.' A few sobs broke out and a hushed murmur went round the cave. He had to think fast! Once again there were desperate creatures looking to him to save them. *I have to get them out of here before it's too late!* he thought frantically. Outside, on the plateau he could hear the Fweens screaming and baying for blood. The moon was climbing and he knew instinctively that something would happen at the moment that it reached its zenith.

'Snoot!' he called out to his friend who having been consoled by his parents was now bombarding them with questions. 'You have to lead them all back to the Cavern! There's no time to lose!'

'But what about you Piper? We didn't find your Voice.'

'There's no time to worry about that now Snoot. We have to get these poor creatures to safety. You go on ahead and lead the way. I'll follow on behind,' said Piper urgently. 'It must be nearly midnight; I don't know what's going to happen but I don't want to be here when it does!'

Snoot quickly took control of the situation and ushered his parents and the rest of the frightened captives out of the cave. The sight of the unconscious beast with its jaws wide open filled them with renewed terror but Piper reassured them that the Vishis Fween would not be waking up any time soon. He waited behind until Snoot and the captives were past the body and safely on their way back to the Cavern of the Thundering Falls, then he took a last look at the prostrate form. It crossed his mind to retrieve Betula but he thought better of it.   She had done her job and Gnawberry would be proud.

Just at that moment the full moon reached its zenith. As Piper looked up into the night sky, he felt again the sensation that had stirred within him as he'd gazed at the moonbow only now it was stronger; more potent.   He marveled at the feeling which was beginning to hypnotize him. A feeling of lightness crept through his body until he was hardly aware of himself. He stood there reeling while the crazed Fweens charged up the mountain towards him. The howling of the advancing wolves came to him as if in a dream. He felt serene and strangely unafraid. Overhead a large yellow bird fluttered and squawked and a flying squirrel shrieked, but Piper hardly registered their presence. He felt at peace as he waited for the welcome and inevitable release.

Seventeen

The Song of Triumph

The tribe of Fweens having hung on long past the appointed hour, was now rampaging up the mountain in search of fresh meat. By this time they were so crazed with hunger that they no longer feared the vengeance of their leader. He had kept them waiting for far too long. Now they were bearing down on the small defenseless Froom who stood in their path.

The moonbow had worked its magic on Piper, making him believe that anything was possible. He had overcome the Vishis Fween and saved the prisoners from their fate. The words of Froshus Ferret sang triumphantly in Piper's head. *If you have courage you'll find your Voice.*

From the pit of Piper's stomach the sensation rumbled. It began low and grumbling and slowly grew in intensity like a gathering storm. It worked it's way up through his body with increasing force until he could no longer contain it. He judged his moment, raised his snout to the moon and opened his mouth wide. Piper's Voice exploded from his throat in one beautiful, pure and perfect note. It was glorious! It was triumphant! It was mesmerizing!

The Fweens were stopped dead in their tracks by the earsplitting force of that note. The body of their leader lying seemingly dead, on the path in front of them stirred their frenzied brains to realization. As Piper's Voice grew stronger and higher, they tore at their heads, screaming in agony until he reached a note so high that it could no longer be heard. The light evening air stiffened to a shimmering, vibrating wall of sound and the hard, impenetrable rock of Mount Florn itself began to crack with alarming report. The loose rocks that had sat comfortably on the summit for so many moons, came tumbling down onto the tortured Fweens who turned tail and fled down the mountain into the path of the advancing wolf pack. They too were suffering some uncomfortable effects from the ear-shattering note though they'd been some distance away.

Piper was reeling from the intensity of his new found Voice as he watched the raving Fweens galloping chaotically down the mountainside. Relief and happiness washed over him and his heart swelled with pride and joy as he thought of the Boodogs and the creatures of the Wide River Valley, and of Loupus and Grizel, and the Beavers and the Ferrets, and of Pa and Ma, and Grandpa; and of course, Pierre.

Then with his new Voice, he began to sing his triumphant song. The notes as bright and as silvery as the full moon's beam, poured from him like honey, smooth and sweet and rich.

Flyyyy, Flyyyy,
By moon's full beam and moonbow bright
Release the Boodogs from their plight
Then fly with haste to woods afar
And drop a note to Ma and Pa
To let them know we're safe and sound
And Soozles both, once lost are found
The evil Fweens are forced to flee

Mount Florn is free from tyranny
Tell creatures everywhere, Rejoice!
For Piper Froom has found his Voice
Rejoice! Rejoice! Rejoice! Rejoice!
For Piper Froom has found his Voice!
Flyyyyy, Flyyyyyy, Flyyyyyyyyyyyyyy!

Piper's final, perfect notes soared out from Mount Florn and flew to the four corners of the land. They rang mesmerizingly in the ears of the creatures of the Wide River Valley and beyond and all who heard them were spellbound.

As Piper made his way back to the Cavern of the Thundering Falls, he marveled at what had just happened to him. The moon was so bright that it cast his shadow on the path ahead. The moonbow had faded away but he would hold the vision of it in his heart forever for he now knew that that was the moment he'd started to believe in himself.

As he entered the Cavern, the scene that met his eyes was one of abject misery and defeat. Snoot was weeping and being comforted by his parents and the Boodogs were slumped on the ground, bereft of hope. The rest of the creatures were sitting hunched and dejected in the corner. At the back of the Cavern in the tunnel entrance, Piper could just make out the humped mound of the Greavil who was still sleeping peacefully.

Of course! he suddenly realized. *With the roar of the Falls they won't have heard my song!* Piper stood silhouetted against the thundering cascade of water which gleamed luminously in the full moon's beam.

He began to sing, softly at first, then stronger and stronger until the lovely notes reached an exhilarating crescendo, drowning out the roar of the Falls, filling the Cavern with the sweet and wonderful sound; and then Snoot was crying and hugging him. The Boodogs, the Soozles and the creatures were crying and hugging each other.

'Oh Piper! We thought you were dead!' Snoot yelled.

Piper looked around at the tear-streaked faces which now beamed with hope and expectation. 'You're free!' he shouted.

Eighteen

That Famous Night

No one slept that night. That night that would be talked about for many moons to come, when an old Chisel-beaked Stonepecker led a rescue party of eagles, wolves, ferrets and a flying squirrel to Mount Florn. That night that the ferrets were applauded for their brave part in the Fween rout (for it was indeed Froshus and the boys who rounded up the deranged runaways and delivered them to the wolves). That night that Mr Eagle earned the respect of Mrs Eagle, Snoot Soozle was reunited with his missing parents and the captive creatures found their release. That night that a flying squirrel threw a small, white stick to a courageous Froom, an act which was to save the Boodogs from extinction and secure the future for creatures far and wide. That most famous of nights when Piper Froom found his Voice and became a hero.

That night the creatures came from far and wide, some in search of missing loved ones, others to catch a glimpse of the heroic Froom who had single handedly defeated the Vishis Fween. Pierre had spread the word of Piper's brave conquest and the rout of the evil Fweens, and there was great jubilation and celebration.

Oderus had been so overcome at being reunited with his misses and nipper that he'd fainted clean away and had to be revived with one of Patience Ferret's famous tonics. Loupus had beamed with joy at finding his two companions safe and unharmed. 'You learrrn well my hheroic frrriends! I verrry proud wolf! My pack they get rrrid of the Fweens. We take back Mount Florrrn! The poorrr Boodogs can go hhome in peace.'

The Boodogs had been elated to emerge into the sweet, fresh air after such a long and miserable captivity.

'Stay with us,' Mot had implored Piper. 'Make your home with us on the south slopes.'

'Pa needs me,' Piper had replied, shaking his head. 'I have an important job to do.' Mot had sighed and nodded.

'You do indeed Piper, you do indeed.'

Although exhausted, Froshus and the boys were exuberant after their night's work. 'Them Nokshus berries cert'nly did the trick,' Froshus had said loudly, in a vain attempt to hide his emotions, and Grizel had bounced up and down shrieking with delight.

'Well, my fearless, Froomy friend, you might be able to sing but you can't catch for toffee!' she'd said. Piper had grinned with pride and pleasure. They had cared about him after all!

Poor Pierre had been truly devastated by the realization that he was to blame for Piper and Snoot's disappearance. His relief at finding them safe and well was so great that for the first time in his life, he was completely lost for words. He'd just hung his head and squawked with remorse. 'But Pierre,' Piper had said reassuringly, 'if it hadn't been for you and your story, the Fweens would still be terrorizing the creatures of the Wide River Valley, the Boodogs, the prisoners and the Soozles would all have perished, and I wouldn't have found my Voice.'

'What a noble, courageous Froom you are,' said Pierre at last. 'Now Bambino, I must fly. Your family will be anxious for news,' and with that he hoiked up his wings, galumphed clumsily into the air and flew off in a shower of yellow feathers.

As the moonlight faded a faint glow began to spread from the East and the weary creatures started to make their way home. Many moons had risen since the two friends had set out on the quest to find Piper's Voice. Now it was time for them to make the long journey back to the Lumbery Wood.

'Before yer go, my Patience 'as somethin' for yer,' said Froshus.

'It's a new Betula,' said Patience shyly as she handed Piper a small, white stick. 'She's still got 'er bark, see! Betula's 'ard to come by round these parts but me old Ma still 'as one or two in reserve.'

'Thank you,' said Piper with heartfelt gratitude. 'Now I can keep my promise to Gnawberry,' he said as he tucked the new Betula firmly into the groove behind his ear.

Grizel had said goodbye with the rising of the sun. 'I need my beauty sleep,' she'd told Piper.

'Will we see each other again?' he'd asked shyly.

'That rather depends on whether you're planning on jumping out of an eagle's nest any time soon,' she'd joked. Then seeing Piper's crestfallen expression she'd added, 'I'm thinking of moving on anyway.' He'd bowed his head to hide his disappointment.

'No!' she'd said emphatically. 'It's pastures new for me. I've heard there's a nice little place called the Lumbery Wood with tall trees and a Wide River. That sounds like it would suit me just fine! But right now this flying squirrel has to fly,' she'd said, taking off before Piper had had a chance to respond. He'd tried to remain dignified but the smile on his face left no doubt as to his feelings.

Snoot too could hardly keep from smiling. He'd found his parents. As they journeyed homeward there were many stories to tell. Piper and Snoot had been wide eyed and agog at Cracker and Stasha's story of how they'd been swept away by the flood waters on the night of the Great Storm.

'We thought we were done for,' they'd said. 'Then the river threw us up, far from home and we were too exhausted to make it back. We had no choice but to dig in and wait for spring. Then the Fweens came and dragged us from our burrow. We were terrified and we thought we'd never see you again.' Stasha had sobbed wetly into Snoot's fur. 'Imagine our surprise when you two appeared in the Vishis Fween's cave!'

Now they were nearing their journey's end and they came at last to the banks of the Wide River where all their adventures had begun. The dam was in perfect order as promised.

'It seems like a lifetime ago that we were on that far bank wondering how to get across,' mused Piper.

'And here we are on the other side looking back,' reflected Snoot. Cracker and Stasha too were quietly reliving their own memories of the Wide River.

As they gazed in silent contemplation at the deep, still water the surface was suddenly broken by four small, whiskery heads which popped up simultaneously. A moment later Gnawberry and Gnawra popped up alongside them. 'Well I never! Piper Froom and Snoot Soozle! And you must be Cracker and Stasha,' said Gnawberry excitedly. 'Pierre has told everyone the news of your homecoming hasn't he Gnawra?' The four small heads swiveled and bounced up and down in the water.

'Is that him Pa, is that Piper?' they all demanded at once.

'Now then young kits, remember your manners,' said Gnawberry to his new offspring.

'How-do-you-do Mr Piper and Mr Snoot and Mr and Mrs Soozle,' said the kits in unison.

'We all do very well thank you,' laughed Piper. He reached up and plucked the new Betula from behind his ear. 'You were right about Betula, Gnawberry, she was lucky and she did keep us safe but we couldn't bring her back. I have a new one though, complete with bark,' he said as he handed her over.

'Well bless me!' exclaimed Gnawberry excitedly. 'Look at that Gnawra! Complete with bark. Now you can stop worrying about the little chaps becoming ill. But are you sure you won't be needing her, Piper?'

'It looks like you're going to need her more than I do,' laughed Piper as he watched the kits bouncing up and down on Gnawberry's head. 'Besides, I have all the luck I could possibly want. You were wrong about the ferrets though Gnawberry. They're not sneaky little blighters at all! In fact they're very brave and kind and funny. It was Patience Ferret who gave me Betula.'

'Well, I suppose I might have misjudged them,' Gnawberry conceded. 'After all, it's thanks to a ferret that *I'm* still here!'

The sun was beginning to set as the weary travellers said goodbye to the Beavers and crossed the dam. They were finally back in their beloved Lumbery Wood and the last leg of their journey was made in contented silence. All had been said and done. They were home at last.

Outside the Soozles' burrow Piper parted company with Cracker and Stasha who were eager to get settled in. Snoot stood by a little sheepishly, reluctant to part from his friend. 'It seems strange to be going our separate ways after all this time together,' he said.

'I'm not going far,' said Piper gently, 'and we'll see each other tomorrow. We'll pick up where we left off,' he added, laughing. 'It will seem as if nothing has happened.' Snoot grinned knowingly at him. They both knew that nothing would ever be the same again.

Piper's head was full of thoughts and emotions as he approached the Froom burrow and his journey came full circle. Then they were upon him, Ma, Pa and Grandpa, soaking his fur with their joyful tears, hugging him tightly, afraid to let him go while just above their heads a big yellow bird squawked his own heartfelt welcome to the home coming hero.

Nineteen

The Spring Wake-up Song

Piper Froom opened his eyes, poked his long velvet snout from his cozy bed of leaves and sniffed the air. Spring had crept into the Froom burrow and tickled his nostrils with her warm breath. He lay for a moment listening to the rhythmic snoring of Ma and Pa in the next chamber as his mind drifted back to last spring when he had been a timorous young Froom who couldn't sing. Today was his day. The honour of singing the Spring Wake-up Song had passed to him, Piper Froom. He would make Pa proud. He climbed eagerly out of bed, stretched out his stiff little legs and set off to climb Noggin Hill.

The Lumbery Wood lay stretched out below him, the tender young shoots of the tall trees shivering in the frisky breeze. The birds had ceased their morning chorus and were waiting with bated breath, for today was the day. Piper breathed in the fresh new day, raised his snout to the sky and let the jubilant notes fly, far and away.

Spring is here,
Spring is cheer,
Twister your whiskers
Untangle your hair
Frisker your tails and twingle your toes
Come out and sniff the new blown rose
Wake up, get up for Spring has sprung

126

Trimble your trotters, come join the song
Patter your paws, come sing along
For Spring is now and Spring is cheer

Over the Woods they flew and across the Drumlin Hills where the Spring breeze picked them up. She carried them across the Flornean Plain, she sprinkled them onto the Forest of Mustela, she swept them lightly over the Densim Pass, then with one last breezy blow, she puffed them gently down onto the summit of Mount Florn.

Spring iiiiiiiisss heeeeeeeere!

The End

Lightning Source UK Ltd.
Milton Keynes UK
UKOW050337171111

182196UK00001B/27/P